THE KENTUCKY WAY

John M. L. Brown

ISBN: 153986006X
ISBN 13: 9781539860068

To Faye

CONTENTS

AUTHOR'S NOTE

This book is a work of fiction set in Crittenden County, Kentucky, where I was born and brought up. All of the characters in the book are fictional except for my great-uncle Bill Lowry, who I am sure would not object to his cameo appearance. To my knowledge, there has never been a political boss such as Ross Taylor or any kind of a large criminal conspiracy in my county, so I had to create such a person and invent such a criminal enterprise in the hope of making the book a good read. Any resemblance in the book to actual persons or events is purely coincidental.

CHAPTER 1

SEPTEMBER 1947: INCIDENT AT THE MAUDE ALICE MINE

The night shift was over and I was nearly home when Dad's hoarse voice came over the two-way. *"Gene, where you at?"*

I picked up the microphone. *"I got off work half an hour ago."*

"Well, then you'll get some overtime. Pick me up in front of the courthouse."

I slid the patrol car around in the gravel and headed back toward town. I spotted him there on the sidewalk, squinting into the morning sun, carrying a big paper cup that looked to be a malted milk from the soda fountain across the street. Snatching open the passenger door, he set his cup on the floorboard. "Gimme the keys," he said.

When I handed him the key ring, he hustled around and grabbed my rifle out of the trunk, laid it on the back seat, and tossed me a box of cartridges.

"Where to?" I said, as he jumped in and slammed the door.

"Deacons Landing."

I put the car in gear and popped the clutch, hoping he'd spill his malt, but he was too agile for me. As we headed out South

1

Main, I glanced over at him and said, "How come you're wearing your uniform instead of a suit of clothes?"

"How come you don't tend to your own business?"

"Well, Dad, I just can't help myself. What's going on down at Deacons Landing?"

"Riot at the Maude Alice mine, shots fired, phone lines dead."

"So what's the plan?"

"Don't know yet. A fellow called it in from that little store where the Maude Alice Road comes into the highway. He was up at the mine when the wheels come off the wagon. We'll talk to him first and then we'll make a plan."

When I braked for the Crayne Hill curve, he leaned over and frowned at the speedometer. "Son, there's a dog over here pissing on your tire!" This was his crude way of telling me I should drive faster.

In the parking lot of the country store sat an old Caterpillar crawler with one of those overhead cable-operated blades. We were walking toward the store building when a man came out the door and met us on the porch. He was eating a Hershey bar. "Hi, Mr. Taylor," he said. He didn't seem all that upset.

"Hello, Howard," Dad replied. "This here is Gene."

"Hidy."

I started to respond, but Dad was impatient. "All right now, what's going on up there at the mine?"

Howard swallowed the last of his candy bar. "I brought my dozer out here this morning and just got it backed off the trailer when it all started. They hired me to build up the approaches to a new set of scales there by the office, you know, and do some other work there on the—"

"Howard, I need you to get to the point."

"Well, *hell*, I'm telling it as fast as I can. What I was about to say is, a passel of the men on the morning shift are Watkinses from down around Willow Sinks. You know, brothers and sons and cousins and in-laws."

"Yeah, I know some of them Watkinses."

"Yeah, well, *to get to the point,* Old Man Ambrose Watkins goes up to the office and knocks on the door and goes in. Do you know him? He spells his name like *Ambrose,* but he pronounces it like *Ambers.* He's—"

"Who all was in the office?"

"Mr. Helton and Mr. Slack and Miss Peggy Wilson. They're the new owners and she's the bookkeeper. Helton's a paper pusher and Slack's the mine superintendent. Anyhow, in about a minute Old Man Ambrose comes flying out the office door like he's been shot out of a cannon and he tumbles down the outside stairs and lands flat on his back. Then I see Mr. Slack standing in the doorway dusting his hands like he's just done a good job of work."

Dad raised an eyebrow. "Well, I reckon that set the haystack afire!"

"That's what I thought, too, but I didn't have sense enough to get my ass out of there. Just sat there and waited to see what happened next."

"So what did happen?" I said, earning myself a pitiless stare from Dad for interfering with his investigation.

"Finish your story, Howard," he snapped.

"Okay, so the old man picks himself up and hobbles off towards the parking lot like he's really got something on his mind, and some of his relatives are sidling over thataway too. Some of the other miners decide all at once to take the rest of the day off—rats and sinking ships, you know—so their cars and trucks go scratching out of there throwing gravel everywhere. Them that didn't have a car took off afoot. About the time all this is happening, I can see Mr. Helton peering out the office window and I remember wondering if him and Slack know just how bad things was fixing to get."

"Well, they're a couple of morons."

"You're mighty right about that! Anyhow, when the old gentleman comes back from his car he's carrying some kind of a double-barrel blunderbuss, and he cocks the hammers and cuts loose, BOOM-BOOM, right into the front window of the office. I think Helton saw it coming and got out of the way. Then Slack or Helton, one or the other, sticks an automatic pistol—looked like a German Luger—out the busted window and blazes away. I don't think he took aim or nothing. Probably had his eyes shut." Howard was scornful of the amateurish pistolcraft.

"Was anybody hit?"

"Not that I know of, but one round pinged into the dozer, so I spun her around and put the blade up as high as I could between me and that pistol and backed down the road till I got to the store. I can show you the bullet mark on the side of the dozer if you want to look at it."

"Not right now. Who was it fired that shot?"

"If I had to guess I'd say it was Slack, cause he's a tough guy. He thinks he is, anyways."

"Are you in a hurry to get on back up there to finish your job?"

Howard shook his head. "Not today, thanks all the same. The old lady's on her way out here to pick me up. My truck and trailer can stay right where they're at up at the mine, and the storekeeper said I could leave the dozer in his parking lot over the weekend."

"Do you want to press charges against whoever fired that shot at you?"

"I guess not, unless you tell me I ought to."

"It's strictly up to you, son."

"Well then, I reckon I won't," Howard said. "I don't think anybody shot at me a-purpose."

It wasn't long before Howard's wife—a sinewy country girl manhandling a battered war-surplus Dodge pickup truck—showed up to take him back to town. We went in the store after he left, and I assumed I was fixing to find out what the plan was.

A neat little man came out from behind the counter. He was wearing a neat little white shirt and a neat little black bow tie. "Got some excitement up the road, ain't we, Sheriff?" he said.

Ignoring the neat man's comment, Dad said, "Looky here now, I need a case of cold drinks and a bunch of salted peanuts."

"Will that be cash money, Sheriff, or do I send the bill to the county and pray to God I get paid someday?"

Dad's eyes narrowed. "Cash money if you can get my order filled in time for Christmas."

The man made a prissy face and looked insulted, but he went to the drink box and took out a bunch of Cokes and Nehis and Seven-Ups. Then he went back to his storage room and came back with a cardboard box filled with little bags of Planters Peanuts. "How many of these was you wanting, Sheriff?"

"About twenty-five bags ought to do it. What do I owe you?"

After Dad settled up with the neat man, we went back outside and put the cold drinks and the peanuts in the car. "I'll drive and you get your rifle ready," he said. "We'll just ease on up there nice and slow, with the red light flashing but no sireen."

I had the jitters. "How do you see this playing out once we get up there?"

"If nobody's been killed or hurt very bad, I aim to hoodoo 'em all into signing a peace treaty everybody can live with. If we don't get this thing squared away today, them bozos are liable to bring a big jug of whiskey and a big jug of coal oil up here tonight. Then they'll drink either the whiskey or the coal oil—it don't really matter which one—and use the other one to start a fire, and that'll be the end of operations for the Maude Alice Mine."

I reached across and took my rifle off the back seat. I threw the cocking lever to chamber a round, topped off the rotary magazine, and shoved a big handful of .250 Savage cartridges into my britches pocket. A fellow can never have too much ammunition.

I was still nervous about what we might be getting ourselves into. "Hey, if Mr. Helton and Mr. Tough-Guy Slack are still here tonight, it may be the end of operations for them and for us too. Maybe we ought to radio Jess and get him out here with some reinforcements."

"Nah, we've got me to do the talking and you to shoot anybody that needs to be shot, so we don't need Jess. Besides, this ain't his kind of a situation."

I knew what he meant. My older brother Jesse was the chief deputy, but about all he did was play big-ass Pete around the courthouse. Sometimes he'd drive out through the county serving summonses and subpoenas in civil lawsuits, but he hardly ever arrested anybody. When he remembered to carry a weapon at all, he stuck a little underpowered .32 popgun in his waistband, so it was obvious that an uprising of angry miners was not "his kind of a situation." In fact, he really didn't care much for *any* of the hurly-burly of county law enforcement. At one time he was a great college athlete, but now he had a gimpy leg and the beginnings of a belly. He'd have to watch out as he got older or he'd end up a big tub of guts.

It was about half a mile from the highway to the mine. When Dad and I drove up, I could see the office off to the right with its blown-out window and some armed men back to our left who were obviously laying siege to the office. We got out of the car, me with the rifle slung upside down behind my left shoulder. Dad walked to the front of the car and raised his voice where everybody could hear him.

"I'm Sheriff Ross Taylor," he said. "A lot of you all know me, and I reckon most of you voted for me. This young man here with me, in case you don't know him, is my boy Eugene. He killed about ten thousand Eyetalians and Germans during the war, but he ain't been quite right in the head since he come home. I'm a little leery of him my own self."

I felt my face burning with embarrassment, but he wasn't finished by any means. From about six feet away, he bellowed at me like I was a half-wit: "Now, Eugene, I want you to take up a position right over there by that front fender and keep a close eye on everybody. And for the love of God, don't let your gun go off by mistake."

"This rifle don't go off by mistake!" I hissed.

Under his breath he said, *"I know that, but them Watkinses don't know it! Now I want you to shoot anybody that looks inclined to hurt you or me or that woman bookkeeper. You can use your own judgment on everybody else."* Then, walking over toward the Watkins battle lines, he sang out, "Roughhouse Watkins, are you over there somewheres?"

"I'm over here," said a raspy voice.

"Are any of you all interested in causing harm or injury to Miss Peggy Wilson over yonder in that office?"

"No sir, we ain't got nothing against Miss Peggy."

"Mr. Ambrose Watkins, where are *you* at?"

"Here," said an old-man voice from behind a pile of scrap lumber.

"You ain't mad at this nice lady, are you?"

"No sir. Far as I'm concerned, she can come on out of there if she's a-mind to. I weren't a-shooting at her, nohow."

"I want her to come out to my car and get herself a Co-Cola and a sack of peanuts. Then she can sit there in the front seat while everybody else enjoys a refreshing cold drink and some tasty salted peanuts. And I mean *everybody*, including them men you've got hemmed up in that office."

"Well, I don't know about that, Sheriff."

"Mr. Ambrose, I'm afraid that's the way it's got to be, so let's don't fuss about it. Now you all hold your fire while we get Miss

Peggy out of there." He looked over his shoulder at me and bawled, "Gene, you be sure and keep a good lookout." Then he made a megaphone out of his hands and yelled up to the office, "Miss Peggy Wilson, can you hear me?"

"I can hear you, Mr. Taylor."

"Ma'am, are you a-scared to walk out here?"

"I'm *awful* scared, but I'm coming out. Tell Mr. Ambrose and them not to shoot me."

"They ain't about to hurt you, Miss Peggy. You come along now."

While all the palaver was going on, I was studying the lay of the land and looking for whoever might become a problem if everything all of a sudden went to hell. I couldn't see any sign of the two heroes in the office, so I figured they were busy keeping their heads down. As far as I knew, neither one had anything more potent than a pistol.

All of the Watkinses appeared to be armed with old shotguns or two-dollar pistols, except for one mean-looking fellow about my age who was sitting cross-legged on a little rise overlooking the whole battlefield. I knew him. His name was Alton Watkins and he was holding what looked like a little .30-caliber M-1 carbine that most likely came home from the war in pieces hidden in somebody's duffel bag.

I recognized Alton because a few months earlier I had arrested him for hurting a fellow in a Deacons Landing poolroom fight. I caught his eye and gave him what I intended to be a steely glance, mentally marking him down as my first target if everybody started shooting again. He was looking hard at me too.

If a fight commenced, I intended to lose no time in putting some cover between Alton and me. Once I did that, he'd be in some serious fucking trouble if he was still where I could get my sights on him. Nerves and jitters had never stopped me from busting a fellow wide open with a rifle ball if such a thing became necessary.

In the meantime, Miss Peggy Wilson had peeped out the door and was now heading across no-man's land toward the patrol car. She was a slim, attractive older woman of thirty-five or forty, and it looked like she'd just applied a fresh coat of dark red lipstick. As she approached, Dad took the case of cold drinks and the bags of peanuts out of the car and set them on the ground by the passenger-side door. He shook Miss Peggy's hand with great warmth and then handed her a Seven-Up and some peanuts like he was awarding her a grand prize. She looked a little befuddled because the cap was still on the bottle, so I whispered to Dad, *"There's a bottle opener in the glove compartment."*

"We ain't gonna need it," he snarled. *"Now shut up!"* Turning away from me, he made a big show of taking the Seven-Up back from Miss Peggy and then I'll be damned if he didn't haul off and pop the bottle cap off with his teeth! He wiped the top of the bottle off with his handkerchief and handed it back to her with an elegant little bow. I heard a murmur from the Watkinses so they must have been as impressed as I was. From the moment that bottle cap came off between Dad's choppers, there was no doubt in anybody's mind who was the master at the Maude Alice Mine.

"Roughhouse," Dad called, "you come on down here and get some of these Co-Colas and peanuts for your merry men. Eugene'll make sure nobody fires on you from the office. You ain't a-scared, are you?"

In response to Dad's gentle taunt, Mr. Roughhouse Watkins emerged from hiding and walked over to the car. His nickname sure fit him like a glove, because he was one rough-looking son of a bitch. He looked like he'd bloody your nose at a church picnic if you asked him to pass the potato salad. When he got up close, Dad said, "I sure do thank you for being man enough to walk over here. Not everybody would've had balls enough to do that."

Roughhouse laughed and spat between his snaggle teeth. "Mr. Taylor, I got balls if I ain't got nothing else."

Dad ha-ha'd at the amusing remark. "Go ahead and take some cold drinks and peanuts back over there as a treat for the boys. Leave two drinks and about four sacks of nuts for them two men inside."

Roughhouse had gathered up the free refreshments and started to walk off when Dad called him back over, draped his arm affectionately across his shoulder, and talked to him low and serious. "I want you to understand that I'm telling you this as a friend. I like you and your family and you know we go back a long ways, but the next fellow that fires a shot today is a dead man."

Roughhouse looked startled in spite of himself. "How's that again, Mr. Taylor?"

"What I'm trying to tell you is that Eugene here will not hesitate to shoot that trigger-happy individual right between the eyes—Eugene don't miss his mark, you know—and then we'll all be in the stew."

Roughhouse wasn't at all pleased with what Dad said. "Does that apply to them big-shots over there in the office, or just to us working men?"

"Now, Roughhouse," Dad said, with infinite patience, "you know better than to ask me that! It applies to everybody within rifle range, and *especially* to the big-shots." He was being a man of the people here. It seemed that everybody, whether rich or poor, had an equal opportunity to be shot dead by yours truly.

Dad's democratic attitude seemed to make Roughhouse feel better. "Well all right then, much obliged for the cold drinks."

"Tell your Uncle Ambrose I'll be along to see you all in a few minutes. First I'll go see the big-shots."

He walked over to me with a happy little smile on his face. He looked like he was really enjoying himself, which is more than I could say. Suddenly I was struck by a thought and I spoke up. "We didn't give Mr. Roughhouse the bottle opener."

He waggled a forefinger in my direction. "I didn't take them damn Watkinses to raise. Besides, it shouldn't take a bunch of hard-ankle miners a real long time to figure out how to get the cap off a cold drink bottle. And it's something else to think about besides murdering them chickenshit capitalists over yonder in the office."

And with that, he took the remaining soft drinks and peanuts and headed toward the office. He knocked on the door and went inside to talk to the mine owners. When he came out again he walked back to the patrol car and then on over toward the Watkins perimeter, winking at Miss Peggy as he went by. He immediately went into a huddle with Roughhouse and an agitated old gaffer I took to be Mr. Ambrose Watkins. After they talked for a few minutes, the old-timer took off his hat, flung it on the ground, stomped on it, and swore a mighty oath. I couldn't hear exactly what he said, but I could tell it was a mighty oath just the same. He was obviously getting something off his chest.

After a while, some of the other Watkinses began to filter over to join the huddle and before long everybody was laughing at something funny Dad was saying. Then all of them except Alton went and put their guns away. Alton stayed right where he was. I still didn't see any movement at all on the part of the chickenshit capitalists.

Dad took a little notebook tablet and a pencil out of his shirt pocket and handed them through the car window to Miss Peggy. "Ma'am, will you help me out by writing out a little old agreement here? My handwriting's pretty bad."

"Anything for you, Sheriff," she said, looking at him all dreamy-eyed like he was her hero.

"All right, then, call it *Agreement to End Labor Dispute*," he said, and began to dictate a short, informal document. When he was finished, he took it over and let Roughhouse and Old Man Ambrose sign it and then he took it to the office for Mr. Slack and Mr. Helton to sign. He came out and showed the owners' signatures to Roughhouse, whereupon all the Watkinses got in their cars and drove off. Alton Watkins climbed in the back seat of the last car to leave and he was still watching me out of the rear window when it drove away. I was glad to see him go. I wouldn't have wanted to shoot him, and I suppose there was always a slim chance he could've shot me first. He wasn't as ugly as Roughhouse, but he looked like he'd shoot a fellow without much provocation.

Once the dust settled, the two mine owners slunk out and pulled their vehicles around behind the patrol car. Miss Peggy, claiming she was about to have a nervous breakdown, elected to ride into town with Dad and me. I think she just wanted to be in the car with her champion. She elbowed me aside and jumped in the front seat beside him, so I had to climb in the back. When we pulled through the mine gate one of the owners closed it behind us and hung a sign on it: *Maude Alice Fluorspar Mining Co. closed till Monday morning.*

As we pulled out of the Maude Alice Road onto the gravel highway, Dad put his arm across the back of the seat and said to Miss Peggy, "What started this little fracas, anyhow?"

"Mr. Ambrose just wanted to report some kind of a little safety problem with one of the hoists, no emergency or anything, but he comes across a little gruff sometimes, and so Mr. Slack said he didn't need any hillbilly miner telling him how to run his mine, and then Mr. Ambrose said he was mining spar when Mr. Slack was . . . uh . . . *shitting yellow* was the vulgar expression he used. That's when Mr. Slack threw him out the door and down the steps."

Dad shook his head. "Is the man an idiot?"

"He's got a degree in geology but he's not from around here and he doesn't know how to act."

"He really misjudged this bunch, didn't he?"

"Yes he did. When we saw Mr. Ambrose coming with his shotgun, I got down on the floor behind the sofa there in the main part of the office and hoped I wouldn't get shot." Miss Peggy shivered at the thought of the danger she had been in.

"Who had the pistol?"

"It was Mr. Slack. Mr. Helton was trying to root his way under the sofa."

Dad laughed loudly at that image and I thought it was funny too. He said, "Could you actually see what Slack was doing?"

"I certainly could. After the front window was blown out, he ran to his desk drawer and got the pistol and poked it out the window and fired it as fast as he could pull the trigger till it was empty. After that, some of the men outside started shooting back, but that's all the bullets Mr. Slack had. I crawled over to the phone and tried to call for help but the line was dead."

Dad dazzled Miss Peggy with a big Hollywood smile and said, "You were brave as a lion out there. I do admire that in a woman."

"Oh, Sheriff, you're making me blush. *You* were the hero. I never saw anybody handle a mob of rough men the way you did. You showed 'em who was the boss."

It began to look like he and Miss Peggy were in the process of talking up a little get-together for later, just the two of them. It made me mad that they were shining up to each other in *my* patrol car with me sitting right there behind them. I cleared my throat to remind them they weren't alone yet. "Can I see the peace treaty?"

Miss Peggy thrust the document at me without taking her eyes off Dad. I unfolded it and admired her neat handwriting:

AGREEMENT TO END LABOR DISPUTE

This is an agreement made between the Miners and the Owners of the Maude Alice Fluorspar Mining Co., on the 12th day of September, 1947. The parties agree as follows:

First, everybody wants the mine to be safe.

Second, the Owners appreciate it when possible safety problems are brought to their attention.

Third, the Miners understand that decisions regarding the operation of the mine must be made by the Owners.

Fourth, Mr. Ambrose Watkins is hereby awarded the first annual Maude Alice Mine "Safe Employee of the Year" prize, consisting of a week's paid vacation beginning on Monday, September 15.

Fifth, Owners and Miners regret any hard feelings that may have arisen during this labor dispute, and each group asks the other to pardon any offense given during that time. Each group is satisfied with the terms of this agreement, and each affirms that, beginning on September 15, the operation of the mine can continue without any further problems.

The agreement was signed by Helton and Slack and by A. Watkins and R. Watkins.

It must be noted that the so-called "labor dispute" at the Maude Alice Mine really had nothing to do with labor and management. It was just a violent reaction by a touchy bunch of men to a stupid personal insult to one of their relatives. But it was the only time my father ever went out on a call with me, just him and me.

Five days later he was dead.

CHAPTER 2

MOM AND DAD

Mom said she first laid eyes on him back when she was the teacher at Odessa Schoolhouse on the road to Shady Grove. She came home one warm spring day and there he sat on the porch trying to talk her papa into giving him a job. He had an old Gladstone suitcase beside him and he was covered with road dust and sweat. She said he looked like he'd been walking for a while.

Mom was an only child of elderly parents and she and Grandma and Grandpa Coop lived down close to the bridge over Big Piney Creek. Grandpa and Grandma owned a fine farm of about 600 acres, and Grandpa also operated a big steam-powered sawmill there in the bend in the road that's about a quarter of a mile this side of the bridge.

It was on the front porch of the old Coop place that Grandpa introduced my parents to each other. Dad took off his hat and held it in his hands, and Mom said "how do you do" and that was that. She said she was just out of her teens back then, but plenty old enough and smart enough to keep school.

Dad must have been a smooth talker that day, because Grandpa Coop hired him to cut timber and snake it out of the woods and to be an off-bearer at the sawmill when he wasn't doing anything else. He was good at everything he did and before long he was the foreman at the mill. He wouldn't hire a man to work for Grandpa if the man wore a belt or smoked cigarettes, because he didn't want the workers slowing down to hitch up their britches or light up a smoke. He wanted galluses and chewing tobacco only.

All was well for awhile—Mom said she and Dad were just sort of nodding to each other from afar—but one day the boiler at the sawmill burst and scalded Grandpa Coop and he lived in agony for two days with boiled flesh falling off his arms. It was a blessing when he died, Mom said.

Dad wasn't there when the accident happened because he'd taken an ox-wagon load of sawed lumber into Shady Grove. It took three yoke of steers to pull that heavy lumber wagon up the Schoolhouse Hill and he was the best man on the place when it came to working oxen or horses or mules. Mom told us he always blamed himself for Grandpa's death, and that he thought the boiler never would've blown if he'd been there tending to business. Mom didn't know what he could have done to stop it from blowing, but she said that's how he felt.

Afterwards—maybe out of guilt or greed or maybe even out of some praiseworthy motive—he was awfully good to Mom and Grandma Coop. He helped them run the farm and the sawmill, and later he made money for them and for himself by selling horses and mules to the federal government during the Great War. Then Grandma died of the flu and Mom and Dad were both alone in the world for a while.

They finally got married and Jess was born the next year, right after they finished building the big house. Mom said she was nearly twenty-five years old by the time they jumped over the broomstick and she'd already decided she was cut out to be an old maid schoolteacher and lead apes in hell. I thought that was a pretty funny notion, but she said my brothers and I caused her so much trouble that she'd rather lead a whole jungle full of apes to hell than to put up with us. We were never quite sure whether she was kidding or not.

Dad was a born politician, a popular man in the county even before he and Mom got married. He could pick a little on an old fretless banjo and he could always draw a crowd and keep the country people entertained with songs and funny stories. For example, if there were no ladies present, he might tell the crowd he was a member of the Piney Creek Pistol Club—drink beer till midnight and then pistol 2:00. It cracked everybody up.

When he decided to run for public office, Mom and Baby Jess rode everywhere with him in a Model T Ford and helped him get elected sheriff in November of '21. He always held elected office after that.

It should be noted that in Kentucky a sheriff can't succeed himself in office, so Dad just ran for county judge every other term and made sure Mr. Veldo Bernstadt kept the sheriff's chair warm for him. So he was sheriff for four years and judge for four years, then back to being sheriff for four more years, and so forth. He didn't have any formal legal training, so he always claimed he was a better sheriff than he was a judge, but Mom told us he *always* ran the show. She said he was bad to do that.

Mom may have been right when she said Dad was the big boss at the courthouse, but out in the country she was in charge. If my brothers and I didn't do things to suit her, she got after us with switches.

She was a farmer. She looked after our crops and livestock with loving care, and she was hell on any chicken hawk that swooped in looking for a nice pullet out of the hen-yard. She kept a 12-gauge

Stevens double barrel hanging over the living room fireplace and she was a great wing shot.

She loved the brindle farm dog Tuck and he loved her, so she was surprised one time when he failed to come when she called him. A couple of worrisome days went by and I finally found him down by an abandoned tobacco barn, held fast by some rusty fence wire wrapped around his right hind leg. The leg was bloody and smelled rotten and I couldn't get him loose, so I ran to the house to get Mom.

She was equal to the occasion. With a set jaw she grabbed up some wire cutters and a single-bitted ax and started out at a trot across the fields to save poor Tuck. Jess and I were able to keep up but little brother Hack was left far behind, blubbering because we wouldn't wait for him.

When we got to the tobacco barn, Jess and I held Tuck's head while Mom used the wire cutters to cut through a great tangle of wire. Then without further ceremony she took a full swing with the ax and lopped the lower leg off clean. Brave Tuck screamed once and then just rolled his eyes and watched while Mom tied off the stump with some binder twine she took from her apron pocket.

About that time Hack caught up with us and Mom had to explain why we ran off and left him behind and why she was chopping up our dog. Then she scooped up Tuck, who must have weighed sixty-five or seventy pounds, and carried him all the way home. She probably didn't weigh much more than a hundred pounds herself, but she never faltered. That's the kind of woman my mother was. Tough as whet leather.

It wasn't long before old Tuck was pretty near as good as new, and for many years he lived on and performed his dogly duties on three legs. When he died she cried like a baby and planted violets on his grave.

As far as making Jess, Hack, and me behave, Dad didn't much care what we did. He was usually gone in the daytime anyway, and there were lots of time when he'd just rent a hotel room in Marion and not come home at all. He always had a much wider orbit than Mom or us boys.

He never in his life whipped either one of my brothers, but he whipped me once. It's worth telling how it happened just to show how his mind worked.

When he was still living out at the big house most of the time, he bought a handsome chestnut stallion called Ruby Laffoon, the namesake of a certain West Kentucky judge and politician who later became governor. Dad looked mighty proud sitting up there in the saddle with his feet in the irons, looking down at everybody.

I got crossways of him one day after Mom sent me down to pick some blackberries in a fencerow next to the Blackburn Road. I'd already picked a bucketful of berries when I saw him, straight as an arrow, coming up the lane with the new horse stepping high and really covering some ground. There may be no finer sight to see in the whole world than a good rider on board a fast racking horse. It was right then that I conceived the idea to jump out and surprise Dad. It made perfect sense to me at the time. I thought he'd be glad to see me and he'd laugh and maybe reach down and pull me up behind him and let me rack on up to the big house with him and I could be proud too.

My plan was flawed. When I sprang up out of the briars and hollered, old Ruby snorted and jumped sideways and left Dad sitting on nothing but air, so he busted his ass right there in the middle of that dusty road!

He wasn't hurt bad, but Mr. John Lloyd Pruitt was coming along in the opposite direction with a team and wagon and he saw it all. That was the worst part because he nearly fell out of his wagon laughing and pointing. So Dad took his pocketknife and cut off a tree limb and stripped the leaves off it and whipped me so hard he nearly brought the blood, and Mr. John Lloyd got to see that too.

There were valuable lessons to be learned from the Ruby Laffoon incident. For example, you shouldn't jump out of a briar patch right under a horse's nose, and you damn sure shouldn't embarrass a politician in front of a voter. And I guess I also learned that a boy's father isn't always glad to see him

CHAPTER 3

CHRISTMAS 1933

When I was ten years old, I got a .22 rifle for Christmas. After dinner on the big day, Dad said, "Get Bob's sack and take it to him, and carry your .22 with you so he can show you which end the bullet comes out of."

I already knew which end it came out of, but all I said was, "Yes sir. What about shells?"

"Get yourself a box of .22 shorts out of the cabinet, but don't load up till Bob says it's okay. Tell him I said *ho, ho, ho.* I've got to go by and see Shad and Shack and then get on back into town." I found myself wondering what important business he had in town on Christmas afternoon. Probably something only grownups would understand.

Old Man Bob Martin was the fellow Dad wanted me to take the sack of presents to. He lived by himself in a raggedy little cabin alongside the steep crooked road that led through the woods away up on the north end of our property. The mail carrier brought him a government pension check every month, and he worked on our farm whenever he was needed. He eked out the rest of his living by trapping, and gathering black walnuts, and digging ginseng. He and I had been particular friends from the time I was old enough to walk.

Bob was a skilled woodsman and hunter, and he was the best rifle shot I ever saw, except maybe for myself later on. At hog-killing time he was the one who dropped each doomed hog in its tracks with a precise shot between the eyes from a cap-and-ball muzzle-loader he liked to call "Old Smellblood." His choice of firearms was evidence of his eccentric nature, because Crittenden County's taste in small arms at that time ran mostly to modern pistols, shotguns, and .22 rifles.

Dad told me to see if my brothers wanted to go to with me, but they were occupied with their own activities and I didn't want them to go anyway. I found the flour sack that had Bob's stuff in it, two pairs of warm wool socks, a new suit of long underwear, and two oranges.

The sack also contained a quart jar filled with a clear liquid. This item and others like it had been confiscated, Dad told us, from a citizen of the county who had violated the laws of the United States of America and the Commonwealth of Kentucky. It hadn't been necessary, he said, to involve the federal authorities in the confiscation process or, for that matter, even to insist on any state or local criminal prosecution of the wrongdoer, who had promised with his hand on the Bible never to break the law again. In view of the holiday season, he said, the confiscated items were being distributed to selected persons across the county to help with their holiday cheer and to remind them of how to vote at the next election. I had trouble following his explanation, but I figured it must have made sense if he said so.

I added some of my own Christmas firecrackers to Bob's sack and carried the sack into the kitchen. "Mom, can I have some leftovers to take to Bob?"

When Mom was busy, she was not a woman to be trifled with. She pushed her dark hair away from her face with the back of her hand and said, "Well, Eugene, I'm trying to get your father ready to go right now. Where are Jesse and Haskell?"

"Outside somewhere."

"Get them to help you bring in some firewood and I'll get to you as soon as I can."

"Yes'm."

I looked for Jess and Hack but they had wisely made themselves scarce and I had to carry all the wood in by myself. When I finished, I found Bob's food wrapped up and waiting. I put it in the sack and got ready to leave. When my mother saw I was carrying my new rifle she said, "Don't be pointing that thing at anybody, and make sure you're back here in time to do your chores."

"Okay, Mom," I said as I walked out the door. I threw the sack over my right shoulder and I carried the .22 in the crook of my left arm, with the muzzle pointing down. It took me quite a while to get where I was going.

For some reason unknown to the modern world, the front of Bob's cabin faced away from the road. I hooted loudly to announce my presence and was answered by a similar cry from the far side of the cabin. I walked around to where Bob was and found him in his overalls and shirtsleeves, using wedges and an eight-pound hammer to split logs into firewood. He was wearing an old-fashioned flat cloth cap and he needed a shave.

"Christmas gift!" he cried. Out in the country, there's a myth that if you shout out that phrase before the other person does, then the other person has to cough up a present for you. The custom is usually reserved for children at family gatherings, but since Bob had no family I thought it was okay for him to yell "Christmas gift." Besides, I had a sack full of presents for him.

Bob had a wide mouth and he always looked like he was just about to say something funny. He was glad to see me. "By God, Santy Claus has done brought me a new rifle for Christmas."

"It's *my* new rifle. Your presents are in this sack."

"All right then, let's see what old Santy's got in his pack. Hey, hold on just a damn minute here, you don't look like no Santy Claus to me! Where's your whiskers at?"

"I'm just one of Santy's helpers."

We went inside the cabin to see what Santa Claus had forwarded to Bob, who declared himself to be perfectly and totally satisfied with the oranges, the new socks, the long underwear, and the leftovers. He didn't say much about the jar of clear liquid, but I noticed that he handled it with special care. The fact was, as I came to know later, he had a taste for ardent spirits.

The cabin smelled of wood smoke and fried meat and unwashed socks, and it had never known the civilizing touch of a feather duster. Bob took the .22 and turned it over and over, examining it in detail. He put it to his shoulder and sighted it into the fireplace, and then walked to the window so he'd have enough light to check out the bore. He fooled around so long I finally said, "I've shot Jess's rifle before, but I haven't shot this one yet."

"First let's go out in the yard and touch off these firecrackers. Then we'll talk about how to make a rifle do what you want it to."

When we went outside, he held up a firecracker and said, "When I was a boy I used to take and hold one of these between my finger and thumb and light it and let it go off. None of the other boys'd do it."

I found this hard to believe. "You must've had some pretty sorry firecrackers when you were a boy. If you tried that with one of these here, I bet you'd blow your fingers off. Are you gonna do it today?"

Bob hesitated. "I reckon not," he said. "Let's get to business."

We shot up all the firecrackers and Bob did not hold one between his thumb and finger and let it go off, as he claimed to have done when he was a boy. When we were finished, he set in to tell me about rifle shooting. Windage, elevation, sight alignment, breath control, trigger press, follow-through, blah, blah, blah. There was more to it than I thought.

"It sounds hard," I said.

"There ain't nothing hard about it. You just learn to do it right and then you do it the exact same way for as long as you live."

He took some old tin cans and stood them in a line on a fallen beech tree in the woods across the road. With the rifle unloaded, he made me hold my breath and sight at a can and click the trigger and cycle the bolt, time and time again.

Before long I was fed up. "Hey, do I get to shoot this rifle or not?"

"You're gonna get to shoot it, but we're not about to waste good powder and lead on half-assed shots. You remind me of Jess when he wanted to learn to shoot. He wouldn't do a damn thing I told him to and he still can't hit the ground with his hat!"

I thought Bob was making things way too complicated. "Why can't I just rest it on a tree limb or something, and then I won't have to worry about holding it exactly right?"

He took a twist of tobacco out of his pocket and cut himself a plug with his Barlow. "What if you was a cowboy away out in the desert with no tree limb to rest it on, and a big old greasy Indian was fixing to shoot you full of arrows?"

"I guess I'd just haul off and shoot him."

Bob snorted. "Well, you might shoot *at* him, but he'd just laugh at you and take your scalp, cause your shot didn't come within ten mile of hitting him. And the reason you missed him was that you didn't pay no attention when old Bob was a-trying his best to teach you how to shoot."

This comment whipped me into line, and I made no further complaint. Eventually, I got to fire live cartridges at the cans, and I did pretty well too. It seemed that the old man knew what he was talking about. After a while I asked, "Did you ever shoot at Indians out in the desert?"

"No, I never did. In my day, the Indians was pretty well done for. I was in Cuba, though, and over in the Philippine Islands."

"Did you have Old Smellblood with you down in Cuba and over yonder in the Philippine Islands?"

"No, in them days I toted a .30-40 Krag-Jorgensen."

There was something gnawing on me. I said, "Bob, I really like to shoot, but I don't think I want to kill anything. I don't even like it when we kill hogs in the fall."

"You like ham and bacon and sausage, don't you?"

"Yeah, but I feel sorry for the poor old hogs."

"There'd be some slim pickings at the breakfast table if somebody didn't kill the hogs. And what if some fellow was fixing to hurt you or somebody you liked? Would you take care of business or would you just let him go on and cut your head off?"

"I guess I'd take care of business."

"I expect you would too."

I didn't like to talk about me killing hogs or people so I changed the subject. "Who were you fighting over there in the Philippines?"

"Ever who they told us to fight—I was over there two different times, you know— but mostly it was the Moros, little turban-headed outlaws. Say, have you ever heard of old William Howard Taft?"

"The one who was president?

"That's the man! He was a big lardass. Long before he got elected president, he was the U.S governor over there in the Philippines. He was a civilian, not a soldier, and he didn't know nothing. He made a speech and said them damn Moros was his "little brown brothers."

"If they were your little brothers, why were you fighting them?"

"They wasn't our brothers by no means! We used to have a little saying: *They may be brothers to Big Bill Taft, but they ain't no friends of mine.* Their idea of a good time was to get all hopped up on dope and get after us with sharp shiny things.

"Like what?"

"Like barongs and kris swords. Sharp and shiny."

"What's a barong?"

"By God, you're full of questions today. It's a big long knife they use to chop up things or people, like a corn knife only with a sharp point and a heavier blade."

"Did you ever shoot any Moros?"

"Off and on I did, but I was just a soldier boy drawing his pay. *Civilize 'em with a Krag*, is what we was told, and so we done a good bit of civilizing."

"So it's okay to kill people if they're trying to kill you, or if you're a soldier and you're paid to do it?" This was a serious matter and I wanted to get it straight.

"I reckon that's about right, plus sometimes you get a powerful urge to kill a man to get even with him for doing something bad to you or your family. You wake up one morning and realize the world ain't big enough to hold you and him both. It ain't legal, but it's the way we do it in Kentucky sometimes."

CHAPTER 4

POOR DEAD UNCLE BENNY

As we lurch down life's pathway I think it's important for us to know who our kinfolks were and where they came from and how they got here. If we know these things, then we already know a lot about ourselves. Of course we also have to figure out some other things on our own.

Dad was mighty close-mouthed about who his people were and where he came from. All he'd ever tell us was that he was an orphan and he was born away over east of here in another part of Kentucky at a place called Mud Camp. The Cumberland River runs through there on its way down into Tennessee, before it curves around back up into Kentucky and finally runs into the Ohio down at Smithland. He told us nobody raised him, he just raised himself.

There was only one time I can remember that he ever broke down and told us a little bit about his life before he came to Crittenden County. It was a Saturday afternoon and Jess and Hack and I were in the kitchen, trying to stay out of Mom's way so we could listen to a World Series game on the battery-powered radio. Elden Auker was on the mound for Detroit, getting the best of the Cardinals.

The game was nearly over when Dad came home unexpectedly, and it didn't take us long to figure out he was sloppy drunk. He ignored Mom and staggered over and turned off the radio. He said he had to talk to us boys about our Uncle Benny, who we'd never heard of till that very moment, and he herded us through the house and out onto the front porch where we'd be able to pay careful attention to what he had to say. It wouldn't have done a bit of good to tell him we'd rather listen to static on the radio.

Mom banged the pots and pans in the kitchen and we could tell she wasn't happy about him coming home in that condition. Although a practicing Baptist, she wasn't particularly bothered by a little manly drinking and cursing and fighting, but she insisted on moderation and she didn't like it if a fellow drank way too much or took the Lord's name in vain all the time. Dad had drunk way too much.

There was no stopping him once he got rolling with his story. He was too good of a county politician ever to speak with perfect grammar, lest he appear to be putting on airs, but on this occasion it seemed like he really went out of his way to talk like an ignorant hillbilly. Maybe it was how he talked when he was a boy.

He and little Benny was about to starve one time, he told us. Hadn't eat in about three days, so after it got dark they slipped down to the bottoms where some men had been picking corn. It was so black dark he had to feel his way along the down rows and Benny had a little sack and they filled it up with all the nubbins the farmers didn't want, so it wasn't really stealing, and then they run back to their shanty down there at the mouth of Judio and shelled that corn and parched it in an old iron skillet over an open fire and they eat up every grain and washed it down with creek water and it was the best food they ever had.

By now, Dad was pretty worked up. He took his hat off and ran his fingers through his hair. Then he heaved a big sigh and proceeded to tell us how one time they were at one of the timber camps and a big whopsided white oak log rolled over poor little old Benny and mashed his guts out with Dad standing right there and not a damn thing he could do to stop it. After that, he didn't have to look out for Benny no more, or nobody else neither except only himself.

He began to snivel a little, which embarrassed us, for we never would have imagined such a thing was possible. We foolishly hoped that once poor dead Uncle Benny got squashed by the log we could go back and maybe hear the end of our ball game, but Dad had a lot more to tell us.

Like how a town boy bragged one time about how fast he could swim across the river and back, and so they had a swimming race, and Dad—who could (he told us) swim better than Johnny Weissmuller—was already standing on the bank laughing when the boy finally got back over to the Burkesville side, and he called Dad a foul name and Dad hauled off and kicked him in the face while he was trying to scramble out of the shallow water, and the boy's face opened up like a tomato, and Dad took that opportunity to go on down into Tennessee for a while.

He was a raftsman after that, he told us, big damn rafts of logs all fastened together and two hundred foot long, headed down to Nashville, and Dad was the very man who taught Old Man Bigbee how to run a raft at night on that crooked river by clacking two rocks together and listening for the echoes off the bluffs.

Raftsmen had a problem, he said, whenever them little stern-wheel steam packets would just keep a-coming, God damn their souls, hogging the channel and not cutting back their engines, throwing waves that would swamp a raft and the men with it, and one time he stuck an ax in the hull of the *J. J. McConnell*, for all the good it did, when it came that damn close to busting their raft all to pieces while they were straining to work their way around Holleman's Bend.

Another time, he and Old Man Bigbee threw a big piece of hickory whaling into the sternwheel of the *D. M. Lewis*, a Nashville boat that crowded them in the Tinsley bottoms, and splinters flew ever damn where. He said he rejoiced a couple of years later when he learned that the *D. M. Lewis* had struck a snag and sunk at the mouth of Greasy Creek.

At first Dad was gloomy about the late Uncle Benny and then he was mad about the various injustices he'd been telling us about, but all of a sudden he brightened up and took a pint bottle out of his coat pocket and toasted us and, by way of celebration, treated us to his version of a little song he said he'd learned from a fellow down at South Carthage, Tennessee:

Me and Maw
And all our chillun,
Goin' down to Nashville
On the "Benton McMillin."

These four lines were the only words he knew to the song, so he sang them over and over for us till he was sure we knew them by heart.

After he got tired of singing, he sat and looked at his fingernails for a while before he commenced telling us that Mr. Cordell Hull, Roosevelt's Secretary of State, had a good name as a river man down there in Tennessee in the old days, but that he never would've gotten elected to public office in the first place if Dad, young as he was back then, hadn't helped him with his politicking. That was before Dad saw the light and became a Republican, however, and nowadays he wouldn't walk across the road to see Secretary Hull eat a bale of hay.

Dad claimed that he himself might have gotten elected to public office and gone to Washington City later on, when he got old enough, if it hadn't been for that little what-you-might-call a misunderstanding about exactly how a certain smart-alecky old boy got his head cracked open with a kingbolt down there at Brimstone Creek Landing, between Celina and Gainesboro. It was because of that unfortunate occurrence and despite the urging of various Tennesseans, including the county sheriff, that he made tracks out of that part of the country.

After that, he said, he followed the wheat harvests out in the Midwest and all the way up into Canada. He also picked cotton in Texas and worked at a big sawmill on a bayou down in Alabama. According to him, all that backbreaking work helped him realize he didn't want to be a hewer of wood and a drawer of water all his life.

Having decided to live by his wits, he told us, he made his way out here to Crittenden County to find his fortune and marry up with Mom and teach all of us West Kentucky yahoos what was what.

Speak of the devil, Mom came to the door and looked us up and down. "Supper's ready," she said.

Dad was slow to respond. Finally he said, "Too early for supper."

"Well, it's on the table if you want to eat. You boys get washed up."

The food was hot, but Mom was icy and Dad was clumsy and looked like he was about to fall asleep in his plate. We boys kept our eyes down and our mouths shut. There was no dessert. Eventually, Mom put down her knife and fork and said, "Eugene, your father can sleep in the bed with you tonight. Jesse, you and Haskell can share the big bed next to the door."

Dad looked surprised at first, but then he got real mad. "I can sleep in the God damn chicken house if you want me to."

Mom had high cheekbones and dark brown eyes that were hooded like a hawk's, and when she spoke you could tell she meant business. "That would be a *perfect* place for you to sleep, but I don't believe your feet will fit the roost pole. Now you finish up your supper and get to bed, and we'll say no more about it." And that was that. Dad went reeling off to bed and Mom and Jess and Hack and I headed for the barns to take care of the evening chores.

Three days later, Dizzy Dean beat Auker 11-0, and the Cards took the Series in seven games. Dad didn't stop drinking whiskey, but if he ever got looby drunk again I never heard about it. Looking back, I guess he had to take on a big load of whiskey before he could stand to talk about his poor little brother Benny, crushed to death by that white oak log all those long years ago.

CHAPTER 5

POLLY TAWBER AND AUNT SUSIE HUGHEY

By way of contrast, Mom seemed to be enchanted with her family history and she was always telling us who our forebears were and how and when they came to Kentucky.

Her papa was Enoch Coop, she said, and his ancestors were Dutchmen who came into Western Kentucky around 1805. Her mama was called Eliza Jane Hughey before she became Mrs. Enoch Coop.

Mom said our Grandpa Coop, God rest his soul, was a great joker. He used to ask people if was possible to tell a lie for so long that it became the truth. Of course the sucker always said no, such a thing wasn't possible, and Grandpa would slap his leg and say that when he married Eliza Jane he called her his old woman, and he told that lie for so many years that it got to be true.

Eliza Jane's ancestor Robert Hughey was a redcoat soldier during the Revolutionary War, and the Americans captured him at a big battle over in the Carolinas somewhere. He escaped from his guards somewhere in North Carolina, and he was never recaptured. After the war ended, the British wouldn't take him back to Scotland—or else he didn't want to go back—so he married a back-country woman called Polly Tawber and headed into the wilderness. Mom said Polly was most likely an Indian because even the modern Hugheys are dark-complected. Furthermore, she said, the name *Tawber* was probably an ignorant person's way of saying *Catawba,* which was the name of an Indian tribe in North and South Carolina.

According to undocumented family legend, Robert and Polly lived for a number of years in that isolated corner of the mountains where Virginia and Tennessee come together. They had some children, but they all died except for the oldest boy. Sometime along in the 1790s, Robert died as well.

Polly's boy—who was called Daniel Hughey—later told people that on the day his father died, his mother howled at the sky for a few minutes, then wiped her tears and got busy. She secured most of their meager belongings, including her three hens, onto the back of the milk cow, whose name was Eenowah. She carried her late husband's rifle and powder horn. Daniel carried the ax and the kettle and led the cow. Polly also made him carry Tarleton, their ill-tempered rooster, in a sack on his back. Then she set their cabin on fire with Robert's body inside, and she and Daniel left there while the flames were still crackling, moving north and west toward Kentucky.

And so it was, Daniel would say, that he and Polly and Eenowah the cow, Tarleton the rooster, and the three hens took up residence for a while somewhere in the fastness of the Kentucky mountains, but he couldn't remember exactly where. While in the wilderness, he said, they had plenty of milk and butter and eggs, thanks to their traveling companions.

A few years later, Daniel ended up in Western Kentucky where he became Mom's great-grandfather. Polly kept moving farther west, and was last heard from out in the Femme Osage country in Missouri, married to a Delaware Indian named Beaverhead.

As an old man, according to family mythology, Daniel enjoyed showing his grandchildren the scars on his ears and neck where (he told them) Tarleton the rooster—resentful at having to ride in a sack with only his head sticking out—had done his best to peck Daniel's brains out. He also told his listeners that every chicken in Kentucky was descended from Tarleton and the three hens, but even the little grandchildren knew that was a lie.

Of all the tales Mom told, my favorite was the one about Aunt Susie Hughey and the guerillas.

It seems that during and right after the Civil War the guerrillas would ride through and take all your mules and horses, and your chickens if they could catch them, and the hams from the smokehouse, quilts and silver spoons from the house, and anything else that struck their fancy. You had to hide your livestock in the woods if you had time, and then try to move as slow as you could with everything else, because there were usually Union soldiers or militia chasing after the men who were robbing you.

"Aunt Susie was my mama's big sister," Mom would say. "Mama was just a little bitty girl when the guerrillas came through that last time, but Auntie was way up in her teens. About nine or ten o'clock on a cold rainy night they were already in the bed when they heard the horses' hooves on the Piney bridge and then a bunch of roughnecks burst into the house cursing and hollering for Grandmama to strike a light and fix them some supper. Grandmama was a widow woman, and she said all those awful men just scared the liver and lights out of her, but there was nothing to do but get up out of bed and stir up the fire in the cookstove and start making hotwater cornbread.

"Aunt Susie and Mama, they were sent to the smokehouse in their night dresses and bare feet, cold and wet as it was, to cut some ham meat for the men to eat. Auntie had an old butcher knife that'd been sharpened so many times there wasn't much left of the blade, and Mama had a coal oil lantern she was holding up over her head with both hands so Auntie could see what she was doing. Said they were both shivering and shaking from the cold, when all of a sudden they saw a shadow looming over them, and there in the doorway stood a big red-bearded man in a slouch hat and a rain cape, with pistols and dirk knives hanging all over him and his white wolf teeth a-shining in the lantern light. It was the guerilla captain!

"He pointed up at the hams hanging there over their heads—like little dead men hanging on the gallows—and he says to Aunt Sue in a big deep voice like this: *Sis, you and Little Bit here get busy and tote all that meat over yonder to the horses. We'll be needing it on down the road.*

"When he said that, Auntie turned around and showed him that little thin-bladed butcher knife and she says, *Mister Man, right now I'm slicing ham meat, but in about one minute I'm fixing to start in on you.* Said the man looked at her right funny and then commenced to laugh, a great powerful laugh like he hadn't had anything to laugh about in a long, long time. And then he said, *Well, hell, just bring in what you've done got sliced off. We'll get more somewheres else afore daylight.*

"Afterwards, the captain and the his men ate their cornbread and their ham meat and drank their well water like proper gentlemen, and then they rode away towards Piney Fork without stealing so much as a silver spoon from Grandmama. The guerilla captain said it was lucky for him and his men that all the Yankees weren't as plucky as Auntie. He also said he was going to come back someday and marry Auntie, but he never did."

It seemed to me like Mom thought the people in her family tree were a little bit superior to other folks, and her stories got better and better over the years. Even the hard-bitten backwoods squaw Polly Tawber eventually evolved, at least in Mom's mind, into an "Indian princess."

Mom laughed a lot when I was young, but not so much later on. She told us ghost stories and stories about the old blue devil and about headless men dragging trace chains through the orchard, but she always finished up by saying that ghosts and goblins were just a load of malarkey, and that she just told the stories for fun.

CHAPTER 6

THROUGH THE
JAILHOUSE WINDOW

D ad was pretty tolerant when it came to us boys. Other than
the Ruby Laffoon incident, he never laid a hand on me.

One time it seemed like he actually tried to shelter us from
some wrath that was about to set down on us. It was on a Saturday
morning and Mom had let us come into town as a treat. About
midday we found ourselves in Dad's chambers at the courthouse,
and he did not appear to be a happy man. "What in the *hell* have
you boys been up to?"

"Nothing, sir," said Jess, acting puzzled by the question.

"What do you mean nothing?"

"Just nothing."

"Judge, it wadn't within a hundred mile of being nothing," said
the county jailer, Mr. Peedad Manner, who was standing by Dad's
desk with an I've-got-you-now look on his face. "Tormenting a poor
jail inmate ain't *my* idea of nothing."

"That's right, you hoodlums! Now why was you all throwing
rocks into the jailhouse windows?"

"Oh, that," said Jess, pretending to be relieved to know at last what Dad was talking about. "Well, we only throwed rocks into one window."

"Only *one*, you say!" He turned his back to us and we breathed a sigh of relief, but then he whirled around and shoved his finger in Jess's face. "But you all would've got *around* to all them other windows, wouldn't you, if Mr. Manner hadn't captured you?"

"No, sir, we wasn't aiming to throw at anything but that one window."

"Shut up, Jess!" He looked at me and said, "Gene, did you throw rocks at that window?"

"Yes, sir . . . Well, one rock."

"Hack, did you?"

Jess couldn't stand it. "Dad, Hack didn't have a good enough arm to throw a rock all the way from the street to the jail, so he's innocent."

"I thought I told you to shut up!" He leaned over and scowled at Hack. "Did you *try* to throw a rock into the window?"

"Yes, sir, and I d-duh-do so have a good arm." Hack had a stammer when he was nervous or excited.

"So your heart was just as wicked as your brothers', wasn't it?"

"I g-guess." Hack looked bewildered.

"Now we've established the *mens rea*, as the lawyers say, so is there any affirmative defenses?"

By this time we were all confused, so we just stood there looking stupid.

Dad threw up his hands and said, "What I want to know is, why was you all throwing rocks and brickbats into the window of the jail? Gene, you answer me right this minute!"

"Well, the guy in the cell cussed us through the bars and called us little fuckers and said he was fixing to come out there and cut our . . . uh . . . ears off. All we were trying to do was walk past the jail and go down there to Jockey Lot to look at the horses, and this guy lit into us, and we hadn't done nothing to him, and it scared us and—"

"It didn't scare me," Jess bragged.

"Me neither," said Hack.

"Well, it scared *me* pretty bad, and then it made me real mad, so I picked up a nice-size rock and winged it through the bars."

"Did you hit him?" Dad asked.

"I don't know, sir. He howled like he'd been hit."

Jess had an inspiration. "Dad, that's when that jailbird started cussing you and the Republican Party, and cheering for Franklin Roosevelt, and so me and Hack flung some more rocks and pieces of brick at him. I don't know if we hit him or not, but we shut him up and got him away from that window. He didn't have no business talking about you like that."

"Mm-*hmm*," said Dad, who looked like he didn't believe a single word Jess said. "Peedad, what's this man in jail for?"

"Drunk and disorderly. Showed his ass over at the pool hall last night and then puked on one of the snooker tables."

"Sounds like a real Southern gentleman. Where's he from?"

"I think he's from Dark Ford or Ryecroft, over in there someplace. He ain't from around here."

"How many people saw this rock-throwing caper?"

"I don't know, Judge. Quite a few, I'd say."

"Well, I know my office phone started ringing off the hook about ten seconds after it happened. Miss Mary Everett called here twice, the God damned old bladder!"

"Ain't nothing wrong with her that a husband wouldn't cure," Mr. Manner said. "What she really needs is a good—"

"Never mind that, what do you think we ought to do with these thugs?"

Mr. Manner was thoughtful. "That'd be up to you, Judge, but it looks awful bad if you don't do *something* about it."

Dad pulled on his earlobe and pondered the situation. Finally he said, "How about an apology? Do you reckon that'd be enough?"

"I *guess* so," Mr. Manner said, but you could tell he was skeptical. He wasn't going to be happy unless all three of us boys got put in the electric chair over at Eddyville.

So what we did, we all marched across to the jail and went up to the second floor. The fellow that started all the trouble was asleep on his bunk. He had a big swollen place on the side of his face, where it looked like somebody may have hit him with a rock.

"On your feet, there," Dad roared, and the guy opened his eyes and dragged himself over to the cell door. His face was red, his eyes were bleary, and he'd pissed in his britches. You could smell him from ten feet away.

Dad said, "I'm the county judge of this county, and these here are my boys. They throwed rocks at you and now they're real sorry they done it. Will you accept their apology?"

"I don't see why not," said the man, who was no fool even if he was a drunkard.

"Good. They're just as sorry as they can be, and they won't ever do nothing like that again. Now, how would you like to get out of jail a little early?"

"That'd suit the shit outa me, Judge."

"Mr. Manner, get this man ready to be released, please." He turned back to the man in the cell and said, "I'll send somebody up here directly to haul you to the county line. Don't come back into this county again if you can't behave yourself."

We followed Dad back to the courthouse, skulking along behind him and unpleasantly aware that quite a number of townspeople were giving us a hard look.

We went in the back door of the courthouse and Dad stuck his head in the sheriff's office and said, "Dagwood, I want you to go over to the jail and get that snooker-table-puking asshole and drive him out to the Tradewater bridge and dump him out. Tell him to walk across the bridge and keep walking."

"Right away, Judge." Mr. Veldo Bernstadt was serving a term as sheriff while Dad was putting in his time as county judge. He had wattles like a turkey gobbler and his Adam's apple worked up and down as he talked. He was a meek and inoffensive old gentleman, and I think being around Dad made him nervous. Dad had started calling him Dagwood after a character in the funny papers, which wasn't very respectful, but like the rest of us Mr. Veldo just took whatever Dad dished out.

"And you better get a towel or something to put on the car seat, cause he's pee-peed in his pants."

Sheriff Bernstadt wrinkled his red-veined nose at the thought of the pee-pee and then hastened off to do as he was told, while Dad herded us on down the hallway to his judge chambers. Ignoring us, he got on the phone and asked the operator to ring the number out at the big house. We could only hear one end of the conversation.

"Hello, dearest, I've got your criminal sons here in my office. . . It looks like they're not working hard enough out there during the week, is what it looks like . . . Assaulted a prisoner in the jailhouse . . . Hell no, I'm not kidding . . . Gene threw a rock and hit this drunk in the face and Jess and Hack tried to do the same thing . . . How's that? . . . No, Jess is way too big to whip . . . I know you could, but I'm telling you he's too old . . . No, it ain't fair to whip *them* if Jess don't get the same medicine . . . What? . . . Tell you what, since you're so smart, why don't *you* just handle it?" He hung up the phone and gnashed his teeth and looked out the window.

After a while, he turned to us and said, "Boys, your mom says for you all to come on home. She's got something she wants to talk to you about."

CHAPTER 7

THE GREAT SCANDAL

What I didn't know till later on was that Dad tended to stray from the marriage bed. Apparently he'd betrayed his vows for years, but things came to a head not long after the rock-throwing incident when he became embroiled in the Great Scandal of 1935. The *Crittenden County Times*, always a friend of Dad's, cleaned up the incident as much as possible:

TRAGEDY ON THE STREETS OF MARION

The citizens of Marion are in shock following a violent encounter that left one man dead and another seriously wounded. According to eyewitnesses, Harold "Boots" Blankenship, 29, approached County Judge Ross Taylor, 45, and without warning cut him across the front of his body with a large knife. Judge Taylor grappled with Blankenship, drawing a revolver and firing two shots. One of the shots struck an automobile parked behind the courthouse and the other entered Blankenship's left breast.

Blankenship died without regaining consciousness. He is survived by his parents, several brothers and sisters, and his wife Lillian, a former employee of the Taylor Funeral Home.

"The incident, though regrettable, was nothing more than a personal difference between the two men," declared Marion Chief of Police R. B. Fielder.

In those days, Dad was the sole owner of the Taylor Funeral Home, located on the town square facing the back door of the courthouse. During the course of getting rich by embalming and burying people who had voted for him over the years, he got involved in some hanky-panky with Lillian, Harold Blankenship's wife. Harold heard about it, swilled down a pint of cheap whiskey, and set out to get even. What he got instead was a trip to the graveyard.

Sheriff Bernstadt told Mom later that he was in his office when he heard the shots and ran out the door and saw Dad on the sidewalk, eyes blazing, holding a blood-soaked handkerchief over his knife wound and apparently trying to decide whether or not to shoot Boots Blankenship a few more times. "There he lays, God damn him," Dad cried. "Ready for the cooling board."

Dagwood Bernstadt gently took the revolver from Dad and led him across the courthouse square and up the stairs to Dr. Frazer's office, where he nearly bled to death on the examining table. As soon as his condition stabilized, he was taken out to the big house to be nursed back to health.

The publicity following the incident caused great shame in our family. Mom became the object of smug pity, while my brothers and I had to endure the smart remarks of our so-called friends.

Jess and little Hack were inclined to react with their fists, but I generally just walked away. I didn't understand exactly what my father had been up to, but I was sorry he got cut and I wished Mom wouldn't be so angry.

It turned out that Dad's wound was serious and bloody, but no major organs were damaged. As soon as he could get on his feet he forthwith moved his personal property—including the red stone-horse Ruby Laffoon—into Marion and he never again spent the night at the big house.

Mom didn't seem sorry to see him go, but she was awfully grim afterwards. I tried hard to do things I thought would cheer her up, but nothing seemed to help. She had a will of iron and when she was provoked, her gaze could burn the paint off a car fender.

When school started that fall, Dad moved Jess into Marion and installed him in one of the rooms in the living quarters on the second floor of the funeral home. Jess ate with Dad at the hotel, and the employees of the funeral home took care of his laundry. Sometimes he came home to the big house on the weekends and sometimes he didn't. Dad enrolled him as a freshman at Marion High School, where he became an instant success with his female classmates and with the football coach. I heard Dad brag one time that Jess couldn't spell *cat* but he could kick a football over the courthouse. It was easy to see what his priorities were.

In the meantime, Hack and I continued our education out in the country at Shady Grove School, and we thought it wasn't fair for Dad to let Jess live in town and play football and hang around the courthouse like a big shot.

I later heard that not long after Dad moved into town, Lillian Blankenship, plump and cheerful in her black mourning clothes, appeared at the Runnels Chevrolet & Buick dealership on North Main Street with five hundred dollars in cash. In exchange for exactly that sum of money, Mr. W. W. Runnels sold her a new Chevrolet five-window coupe. I was told that Mr. Runnels marveled when Lillian told him that the money came from the proceeds of her late husband's life insurance policy. The Blankenships weren't well known for their financial responsibility.

Regardless of where the money came from, so the story went, Lillian packed up her things and drove her new car up Highway 60 to Evansville, Indiana, vowing that she would never set foot in Crittenden County again as long as she lived.

CHAPTER 8
IRENE MCDOWELL

School was out for the summer and I was missing my girl. I got to see her every day at school, of course, but not so much during summer vacation. She and her family went to our church, however, so after school let out I all of sudden got to feeling extra holy.

One Sunday morning brought a warm west wind that whipped dust through the barns as we went about doing our chores. Jess was home for the summer and moseyed around with us, but he wasn't much of a farm hand. Afterwards, as we headed back to the house, we could hear the distant rumble of thunder on the far side of Riffle Hill.

When it was time to leave for church, Jess got behind the wheel of the old Ford truck, and Hack and I squeezed into the middle, and Mom sat jammed against the passenger door. Hack hunkered between my legs and tried to avoid being clobbered in the knees by the gearshift. Fat drops of rain began slapping into the windshield as we headed down the Blackburn Church Road.

Mom was serious about her churchgoing and she dressed up accordingly. Her hat and Sunday dress had been purchased at a dress shop in Marion, and her black high-heeled pumps had been acquired during last year's shopping trip to Paducah. Jess, already as big as a grown man, wore one of Dad's old suit coats, while Hack and I were in our shirtsleeves and Sunday pants.

When we got to the Blackburn Baptist Church, Jess pulled the truck up close to the front door so Mom wouldn't get wet, and then he took his time picking out a parking place. Concealed from prying eyes by the rain, he sneaked a cigarette and gave Hack and me a drag too. We waited as long as we dared before splashing through the puddles to join Mom in the church house, hoping she wouldn't smell cigarette smoke on our damp clothes.

There was a substitute preacher, a middle-aged fellow with a jack-o-lantern head and black hairs sticking out of his ears. After the preliminaries were over, he really got tuned up and his sermon went on and on, complete with much pulpit pounding and many predictions of eternal damnation for the sinners. The pews were filled with worshipers, and the church house smelled, not of brimstone, but of wet wool and cow manure. I sighed and looked up at the cobwebs on the ceiling and wished I was somewhere else.

Across the aisle from us sat Mr. Cortez McDowell with his pretty wife and his four daughters. The oldest daughter was in high school and the youngest was in the fourth grade and they were all good-looking like their mother. My special friend was the second-oldest girl, Irene, who was a year behind me in school and who was looking less and less like a tomboy the older she got. I stared across at her till she looked at me and gave me a little secret wave. I smiled at her and she wrinkled her brow to tell me to stop showing out in church. I gawked at her some more later on when the other people had their heads bowed in prayer, thinking about her instead of my immortal soul. I was at the big depot in the sky, in other words, waiting to board the hell-bound train.

The sun was out by the time the service was over and the churchyard was steaming when we finally walked out the front door. Mr. McDowell immediately herded his flock into their Model A Ford and chugged off, so I didn't get to talk to Irene. Hack and

I went and got in the truck and sat waiting while Mom talked to the preacher and some of the other church members. We rolled down the windows and fanned the air with our hands so maybe the smoky smell from the pre-church cigarette wouldn't be so obvious when Mom got back in the truck.

We saw Jess talking to a well-dressed girl who was visiting relatives in the neighborhood. She was wearing little white cotton gloves. "He's probably telling her what a big football star he is," I grumbled. After a few more minutes, everybody got loaded up and we headed back to the big house.

After Sunday dinner, Mom released us to do as we pleased. Jess asked if we could take the truck, but she said we could go anywhere in the wide world as long as we went there on foot and the sooner the better so she could have some peace and quiet. Jess wanted to argue with her, but she pointed to the door and said, "Stand not on the order of your going, but go at once."

That's when we decided to hike through the woods and down the hollow on the north side of Pine Knob Bluff and past the Collie Hunt place to pay a visit to Old Man Clawson and his two grown sons. They were all crazy and they were likely to be up to something interesting on a hot Sunday afternoon.

As we neared our destination, we began hearing banging noises that sounded sort of like shooting, but not exactly. When we rounded the last curve in the road, we saw that the Clawsons had not disappointed us.

Old Man Clawson was on the front porch of his house wringing his hands and pacing up and down. His younger son, Victor, lay unconscious in the yard. At Victor's feet stood a blacksmith's anvil and nearby on the grass was a sledgehammer. The older son, Raymond, was looming over Victor, shaking his fist and cursing. As we approached, we heard Raymond say, "Get up from there, damn you, you ain't hurt!"

"What's wrong with him?" I asked.

"There ain't nothing wrong with him, except he's got a big pump knot on his head, and he ain't near the man he thinks he is," Raymond cried, kicking his unconscious brother savagely in the ribs. "Get up from there, I said!"

"Should we throw some water on him?"

"You can if you want to, but I ain't doing nothing for him."

Old Man Clawson, who really was touched in the head, rolled his eyes and looked around the yard suspiciously, like he could see things we couldn't see. Then he tiptoed over to the well and drew a bucket of water, and I took it and threw it on Victor. As Victor swam back to consciousness, we began to piece together exactly what had happened.

In an argument fueled by Sunday morning alcohol and Sunday afternoon stupidity, Raymond and Victor had violently disagreed about which of them was the better man. In order to determine the issue once and for all, they came up with a test. They lugged the anvil and the hammer into the yard, and with a sharp knife they sliced an old sweaty stick of dynamite into wafers. They agreed that each in turn would place a dynamite wafer on the anvil and hit it with the hammer, the idea being that you had to hold onto the hammer when the dynamite exploded. If the dynamite blew the hammer out of your hand, you were a sissyboy and you lost the contest.

Everything went fine till Victor whacked an extra-thick dynamite wafer. He was able to hold onto the hammer all right, but just long enough for it to fly up and strike him between the eyes, knocking him cold. He was therefore unable to continue with the contest and Raymond was the default winner, although he didn't seem very happy about it. In fact, he still acted like he was pissed off about something. As I said, they were all nuts.

Victor was sitting on the porch holding his head in his hands when we left to seek diversion elsewhere. Some years later he went to war as a member of the 38ᵗʰ (Cyclone) Division. He was killed during a kamikaze attack on a troopship out in the Pacific some-where. Afterwards, Old Man Clawson died in the State Insane Asylum over at Hopkinsville and Raymond was killed in a car wreck up in Illinois. End of the line for the Clawsons, but that was a long time in the future.

Later on that same day, we were walking along the road toward home. It was a lot farther that way than cutting through the woods, but we weren't in any hurry and there was always the possibility somebody would come along and give us a ride. As we scuffed along, dodging puddles left over from the morning thunderstorm, Jess decided to stir up some trouble.

"Me and Hack seen you making goo-goo eyes at that little McDowell girl in church this morning," he said.

"Which girl was that?"

"Don't play dumb with us, boy. You know who we're talking about." He elbowed Hack and said, "He knows, don't he, Hack?" My little brother smirked and nodded, delighted that he and Jess were in on a grand joke together at my expense. I wasn't about to get drawn into a big conversation with either one of them on the subject of Irene McDowell, so I just kept my mouth shut.

Jess would not be denied. "Whoa! Now he's sulling up like a possum and won't talk at all. What can this mean?"

Hack was ready with the answer. "Gene's got a girlfriend, ha ha ha!"

"Shut up, you twerp!"

Jess pretended to be shocked. "Now *Eugene,* don't talk to your baby brother thataway. Even a twerp like him can see that little old girl's got a nice little ass on her. Like a little upside-down Valentine, ain't it?"

"I think she's ugly," Hack sneered, "and I ain't a twerp."

I said, "You just don't like her because she can kick a football farther than you can."

"She c-c-can*not*!"

"And you're the king of the twerps."

"No, I ain't!"

I was trying hard to shift the momentum, but Jess just wasn't going to let up. "Hey, what was them things I seen on that girl's chest today?" he said to his stooge. Hack wasn't catching on, so Jess helped him out. "Maybe a couple of carbuncles growing on her chest, like this," he said, indicating with his hands exactly what he was talking about.

"Yeah, car buckles, that's what they looked like."

By this time I'd had a belly full. "You ignorant little shit, you wouldn't know a carbuncle if it bit you in the ass, or a car buckle, either!

"Shut up!"

"You shut up!"

"*You* shut up!"

Jess held up his arm, flexed his impressive bicep, and showed it to Hack. "Hop up on that and crow, Junior," he said. He had sowed the seeds of discord between his younger brothers and he was content.

In spite of what I tried to get my brothers to believe, I was definitely sweet on Irene McDowell.

CHAPTER 9

NOVEMBER 1940:
KATE AND BELLE

Irene and her family lived in an old house on the left side of the road between Blackburn Church and Shady Grove. Her father owned some good bottomland that was under cultivation and some rugged timberland that he couldn't get at with a truck or tractor. It was his need to get his timber to market that caused him to decide it was okay for his prettiest daughter to be seen in public with me.

In the fall of '40, I was a senior at Shady Grove High, but by then Dad had moved little brother Hack into Marion so he could go to the ninth grade and play football at Marion High. I begrudged the way Dad always treated Hack and Jess better than he did me, and all in the name of football. Jess had gone off the year before to play college football at Murray State, but now (thanks to a tough Bohunk linebacker from a rival team) he was laid up at the big house with a white plaster cast on his leg,. His gridiron days were over and there was no need for him to stay in school, so he quit and came on home.

Irene and I were best friends and we thought we were in love, but old Cortez wasn't pleased about her keeping company with one of Ross Taylor's boys. His theory was that the apple doesn't fall far from the tree, and he hadn't forgotten about the Great Scandal of 1935. In fact, he was one of the very ones who sort of high-hatted Mom at church after the scandal made headlines in the newspaper. His bad opinion of me wasn't improved by what he'd heard about Jess's legendary adventures with the opposite sex at Marion High and down at Murray State.

Anyway, on Thanksgiving Day, he rang Mom up to ask a favor. He wanted to hire Kate and Belle, our two big draft mules, to snake a bunch of logs down off the Peter Cave Hill so he could load them on his truck and take them to the railroad yard in Marion. He was afraid his team of horses wouldn't be up to the task because of the rough terrain and the slick logging trail coming down from the top of the hill. Our mules would be stronger, he said, and more surefooted. Mom said yes, Kate and Belle were about the best team of mules that ever stretched a chain, and he could use them for free because we all went to church together and (after all) that's what neighbors were for.

Mom was a good neighbor all right, but I think she also wanted to heap coals of fire on his head for his holy-joe attitude back at the time of the Great Scandal. Killing him with kindness I guess you'd say, though it's for sure she knew how to hold a grudge. Her religion had a good dose of the Old Testament about it, which was okay with me. I liked to read about all that smiting and begetting.

The mules weren't all old Cortez wanted. He wanted a mule driver too. He said he'd like to pay me a dollar a day to work the mules and help load the logs on the truck. Naturally, Mom said I'd be more than happy to help and there'd be no need to pay me, since we were all such great friends.

One can imagine how much I appreciated Mom's generosity with my time, but there was some good news. Cortez also said they'd feed me an early breakfast and dinner at noon, and Irene could help me with the mules. I guess he would've sold her to the King of the Cannibal Islands if it got his logs down off that hill. He told Mom he thought the job would take two days and could we start tomorrow. She said okay, and told him I'd be there by five o'clock the next morning for breakfast.

I went to bed early that night and it took me a while to get to sleep. I was excited about seeing Irene and spending time with her and maybe showing her old man I wasn't such a bad guy after all. I was wide awake by three and down at the mule barn by three-thirty. As soon as I fed and harnessed Kate and Belle I climbed on Belle's broad back and set out toward the McDowells' house. Belle was the lead, or left-hand, mule and Kate was the off mule.

It was a raw morning, misting rain, and a swirly north wind soon found its way down the back of my neck under my rain slicker. I turned my collar up and pulled the earflaps of my cap down and booted the girls along at a little faster clip. I got to the McDowell place just as their mantel clock was striking five.

Breakfast was almost worth the ride. Country ham and biscuits and gravy, scrambled eggs, fried potatoes, sweet milky coffee, and Irene sitting next to me at the table. Part of my pay, I guess. Cortez spent entirely too much time blessing the food to the nourishment of our bodies and praying for the sick and the lame, but at last it was time to eat. I was starving and it was good and there was a lot of it. The old man usually acted pretty sour toward me, but he was a jolly old elf at the table that morning. He was probably faking, but Mrs. Mac was bustling and pretty and cheerful all the time, and I was glad Irene took after her.

After we ate, Irene put on some work shoes and one of her daddy's old denim coats with the sleeves turned up, topping the outfit off with a knitted cap. Even in that rough outfit she looked to me like a Hollywood star. Her sparkly blue eyes and her honey-colored hair curling out from under her cap gave me a fluttery feeling in my stomach.

We walked outside and led the mules across the road and waited on old Cortez to saddle up one of his nags so he could go up to the wood lot with us for the first trip. I gave Irene a boost up onto Belle and I scrambled up behind her so we could follow him up the muddy trail. I *could* have put her up on Kate, of course, but I felt it was my duty to have her ride in front of me on Belle so I could hold onto her and make sure she didn't fall off and hurt herself.

It was about a mile up to where the logs were piled and waiting. I was glad to see the trail followed around the side of the hill instead of heading right straight for the top. If we were to start down the hill later on and the trail was too steep, the logs might get to sliding too fast and run up under the mules and then there'd be hell to pay. You wanted gravity to work for you, but only up to a point.

When we got to the top Cortez said, "You can find everything you need under that tarp over yonder. Some of them logs you'll have to bring down one at a time and some are small enough you can use one for your leader log and hook another one onto it. It's your mules, so you'll know best about how much they can pull. My old horses couldn't pull the hat off your head."

He was ready to put us to work. "I'll help you all get started and then I'll head on down and pull the truck alongside that cutbank there where the road straightens out. I'll have the skid poles ready and we can skid the logs right down onto the truck and soon as I get a load I can take them to Marion while you and Irene keep going back for more."

He went to the nearest pile and used a sledge hammer to drive a J-grab into the little end of a log, while Irene and I took cant hooks and rolled a smaller log right in behind it lengthways. We began driving grabs into each log, linking the two together like sausages. Cortez crawled on his old horse and started down the hill to get his truck squared away and ready.

After he was gone, Irene and I sat down on the leader log for a little rest. Kate and Belle stamped their feet and pulled halfheartedly at some clumps of brown grass at the edge of the wood lot.

"You look pretty this morning," I said gallantly.

"Ha, ha, I look like a witch and you know it."

"You're about the finest-looking witch I've seen all day."

"That may not be much punkins. How many witches have you seen this morning?"

"Well, let's see, there was one under the Piney bridge and then there was a couple more screeched at me from the Blackburn Cemetery, so I reckon you're about the fourth one I've seen already today. And it's early yet."

"I think you've got trolls and boogermen mixed up with witches."

"Nope, they were all witches. I know one when I see one. Now I reckon we better get these mules hooked in and slide these logs on down the hill before your daddy gets to thinking something's going on up here."

She cut her eyes at me and grinned. "What *might* he think could be going on up here?" She was in a lively mood, considering the weather and where we were and what we were supposed to be doing. It was fun to be with her.

We got the last load of logs on the truck at mid-afternoon on the second day, and I was exhausted. It's the most tired I ever was till after I went off to war. I stood in the road with the worn-out mules and the loaded truck while I talked to Irene and her daddy. Cortez had decided he liked me in spite of himself. "Son, here's what I want you to do, if it's okay with your mother. I want you to sit with us at church tomorrow, and then come and eat Sunday dinner with us. Could you eat the old woman's cooking another day?"

I couldn't believe my ears! "Yes sir, I believe I could."

"Well, do you think you've got sense enough to drive that old log truck there?"

"I expect I could hold it in the road." I was cautious because I thought he was going to find some more hard work for me to do for no pay.

"Good. Then after we eat dinner tomorrow, you and this girl can take the truck into Marion and I'll give you the money to take her to the picture show and get you all some popcorn and a cold drink. Just have her home in time for supper."

"Wow, thanks, Mr. Mac."

"When you get into town, what you want to do is cut over to Depot Street and circle around and park down at Jockey Lot. Then you all can walk uptown to the show, and you won't have to be embarrassed about courting a pretty girl in a log truck."

So Irene Mac and I went steady after that. When I graduated from Shady Grove High a few months later, she gave me a necktie as a graduation present. Mom took me to Hunt's Department Store in Marion and bought me a white dress shirt and my first suit of clothes, and Dad sent me a fifty-dollar bill without card or comment.

I was the class valedictorian—it was a small class—and therefore I had to make a little talk at the graduation ceremony. When I was up on the little stage, it made me happy to see Mom and Jess and Hack and Irene and Mr. and Mrs. Mac and Old Man Bob Martin all sitting on the front row smiling up at me.

The day after graduation Bob showed up at the big house with a present for me. It was a Model 99 Savage, an elegant lever-action rifle. "Out west they'd call this rifle a muley," he said, "cause it don't have an outside hammer like a Winchester or a Marlin does."

It was a wonderful present. I knew he'd spent a lot of money on it, and for some sappy reason it made me feel like I was going to cry. I caught myself and said, "Is it a .30-30?"

"No, it's chambered for .250 Savage. The ball weighs about half as much as a .30-30, but that little son of a bitch is moving down-range at about three thousand foot a second. You wouldn't want to step in front of one."

"It's beautiful, Bob. And my initials are carved in the stock!"

"Yeah, I cut them in there in my spare time. And I got it shipped with sling swivels, but the sling I ordered to go with it ain't come in yet."

That was the beginning of a summer that seems now like just a pleasant, distant dream. I worked hard on the farm and Irene and I were closer than ever. We were excited I was going to Murray State in the fall, and we knew she was going to be down there with me the following year. We talked about how maybe we'd get married and be together while we finished up with college. We had big plans, good plans, but I was a college boy for a few months only. Then the Japs bombed Pearl Harbor and the Germans and Italians piled on, and I found out the way I wanted my world to be wasn't the way the world was going to be. Things haven't been the same since.

CHAPTER 10

JANUARY 1946:
THE RUPTURED DUCK

S hortly after sunrise, I humped my duffel bag off the train at the Illinois Central depot in Marion. On my sleeve were various stripes and rockers indicating that I was a senior enlisted man in the United States Army, but I also sported a "ruptured duck" patch that said I was really just a civilian wearing a uniform till I could get where I was going.

I washed my face in the depot restroom, stowed my bag with the ticket agent, and put on my overcoat. I went outside and walked three blocks west on Depot Street, then north on Main. I was an old man at the age of twenty-two and I hadn't been home in nearly three years.

When I got to the town square, I took a seat on one of the loafer's benches in front of the old courthouse and watched the town come to life. People were hurrying back and forth to get out of the cold and some of them stared from across Main Street, but nobody came over to see me. I probably didn't look the same as I did before, but it made me mad anyway.

At precisely 8:00 a.m., Dad appeared at the corner of Carlisle and Main and angled across the street toward the courthouse. He was wearing a black overcoat and a narrow-brimmed hat with a guinea feather stuck in the hatband. He looked old but he was still ramrod straight and he still had his John D. Rockefeller go-to-hell walk. He saw me and cocked his head and kept walking my way, and I sat and watched him come. It was hard to tell what he was thinking.

When he got closer, I stood up and said, "Hey, Dad," and he shook my hand and said, "Hey there, let's get in out of the cold." He led the way into the courthouse and unlocked the sheriff's office. I followed him in, catching the smells of coal smoke and tobacco juice and floor polish. He pointed toward a chair in front of his big desk—he was serving as Sheriff again— and I took a seat.

When he took off his coat and hat I saw he was wearing a dark brown suit of clothes and a white shirt with a red necktie. There was a bulge under his suitcoat, betraying the presence of a large revolver. His hair was reddish-gray and combed straight back from his forehead and he had a big toothy smile that made him look a little bit like that Massachusetts bootlegger who used to be ambassador to England.

He poked at the potbellied stove and dumped in a few pieces of coal, then fiddled with the damper for a while. Finally, he turned around and looked at me over the top of his specs and said, "If you'd let somebody know you was coming in, we would've had a crowd waiting. The high school band's been down to the depot a bunch of times for boys that didn't do half the stuff you done overseas."

I shrugged. "I just came up here to say hey, and see if I could get somebody to take me on out to the big house, you know, to surprise Irene and Mom."

The stove was putting out a lot of heat and I was starting to feel stifled. I took off my overcoat and threw it over the arm of the chair next to me, and immediately I could see a question forming in Dad's head. "Why, hell, boy, you ain't even wearing your decorations. Don't you know the people love a war hero?"

"To tell you the truth I don't much care what the people love. I just want to get home and see my wife."

That wasn't what he wanted to hear. "First let's just walk around town for a little while so you can shake hands with some folks you ain't seen in a long time."

"Dad, I ain't seen Irene in a long time. Do I have to hitchhike out there, or what?"

"No, Goddammit, I'll call Jess and get him to take you. Me and your mom ain't cordial. You remind me a lot of her, in case I never told you that."

"I appreciate the compliment. It's the nicest thing you ever said to me."

"I want you to come back into town tomorrow and wear your uniform and all of your decorations and campaign ribbons."

I was pissed off that he hadn't even said welcome home or anything. In fact, it seemed like he just wanted me to help out with his politicking, so I stood up and said, "Tell Jess I'll wait for him out by Mr. Lowry's office." I walked out into the hall and through the front door of the courthouse and headed across the yard toward the little building that housed the County Clerk's Office.

He came out behind me and stood on the portico with his hands on his hips. I thought he was going to call me to come back so he could apologize, but when I looked over my shoulder at him all he said was, "Dave Peterson's the clerk now. If you want to find Mr. Lowry, he's working over at the Farmers Bank." I just kept walking.

It was good to see old Jess, who had the siren and red light on as he came around the corner on two wheels and threw open the passenger door. He leaned over and cried, "Get in this car, soldier boy!" I got in and endured his brotherly pounding and it made me feel good to see him happy I was home. We drove out by the depot so I could pick up my gear, and then we headed east on Highway 120.

As we rode out the highway, Jess kept his mouth shut while I soaked up the look of the familiar rolling hills in the weak winter sunshine. Patches of snow dappled the fields, and the cedar trees were almost black in the fencerows. After we turned onto the Porter Mill Road, there were steeper hills and darker hollows and fewer houses and fields.

As we got close to home I made Jess stop the car for a minute under the brow of Pine Knob Bluff. Across the bottoms off to my right I could see a line of bony sycamores marking the course of Little Piney Creek, on its way to join Butler Creek to become Big Piney. I got out and walked around to the driver's side and looked up at the overhang of the bluff. As I turned back to the car I said, "You know, I thought about this old bluff a million times when I was overseas. It's like the center of the world for me." Jess nodded solemnly, like he knew what I was talking about, but he didn't.

Then it was time to go on around the road to the big house, and I realized my hands were shaking and my mouth was dry. I was scared because I didn't know how I was going to act, and I damn sure didn't know what to expect from Irene and Mom and Hack. I didn't think anybody was going to do anything bad—I just didn't know.

Irene McDowell Taylor was and still is the finest woman the Good Lord ever let breathe. We got married when I was home on leave in early '43 because we wanted to love each other like man and wife before I shipped out. We were both virgins and we fumbled our way through a quick honeymoon and then for me it was back to Fort Bragg, and Camp Edwards, Massachusetts, and New York City, and then away and gone.

After I left, Irene moved her things to the big house and helped Mom and Hack run the farm. She had all those sisters, so her dad and mom got along nicely without her. She wrote me a letter nearly every day, and the best thing about the whole damn war was having a mail clerk hand me a batch of letters from her postmarked *Shady Grove, Kentucky.*

But I'm getting off the subject.

Jess started the car and we drove the last mile to the big house. When we got close, he put on the siren and the red light and laid on the horn. I was glad to see that Whitey, old three-legged Tuck's replacement, was still alive and still rushed out to menace intruders. And there was Mom on the kitchen porch, shading her eyes and trying to see what all the racket was about. Hack, now a great tall galoot, appeared in the door. He turned and said something to somebody back inside the house, and then there she was! She came at me in a rush, all blue-eyed and curly-headed, and then she was all over me with her arms around my neck and her legs around my waist, laughing and crying and damning me for not letting her know I was even back in Kentucky, much less in Crittenden County! I'll admit I was crying too.

She realized suddenly that the leg lock around my waist might look a bit indecent, so she let me go and blushed prettily and smoothed out her dress. Jess stood there grinning like he was the one who deserved the credit for making it all happen.

Then Mom came up crying and hugged me, and over her shoulder I could see Hack with his hands in his pockets, hanging back and trying to decide what was the right thing for him to do. I figured he was feeling bad about the bogus farm deferment that kept him out of the service, so I said, "Come here, boy, and let me look at you!"

He sidled over and I grabbed him and looked up into his face and said, "Why, damn you, Hack, you've grown off and left me. How tall are you now?"

"Six t-t-two."

"Well, now you and Jess are both up there where the air's thin. That's why neither one of you has got good sense." This was my way of telling him I didn't give a damn about his draft deferment, I was just glad to be home. He looked relieved and grabbed up my duffel bag and led the way into the house.

Then there was an avalanche of ham and eggs and biscuits and coffee, and everything was funny and everybody was happy including me. After I ate, Jess said, "Mom, why don't you and Hack get your coats and hats and I'll drive you all over to Mr. Hubbard's store so you can lay in some more supplies for this starving boy. And if Mr. Hubbard ain't got everything you need, I'll take you on into Marion." He positively leered at me and said, "Probably take us two or three hours to find it all."

Mom looked just like I remembered her, except for a few fine lines around her eyes and some streaks of gray in her hair. She still looked as resolute and independent as Mammy Yokum, even though she was over fifty. Glancing at Irene and me, she turned to Jess. "That's a grand idea. Eugene needs some new clothes so he won't have to wear his uniform ever again."

Hack said, "If it's okay, I'll stay here and talk to Gene."

"It is most certainly not okay. These old married folks need some time to get themselves reacquainted."

"Oh." He hadn't thought about that.

After they left, I looked at Irene and she looked at me. She said, "I bet you're worn out. Wouldn't you like to have a nap?"

"Yes I am . . . I mean I would. . . uh . . . would you like to have a nap too?"

"Yes."

It was cold in the front bedroom because the fire in the fire-place had died down during the day. Irene grabbed a flannel nightgown off the tall headboard of the feather bed and disappeared into another part of the house, while I built up the fire. When she came back she was carrying her clothes and wearing the nightgown, along with a pair of white socks to keep her feet from freezing on the cold wooden floor. She tossed me a pajama top that must have been Hack's because the sleeves were so long, and she said, "Maybe you won't be needing the bottoms."

I was shivering from the cold and from nervousness and I didn't know what to do next. She padded over, put her hand on my arm, and smiled at me with overwhelming sweetness. "Husband, just go on over there by the fire and take your uniform off," she said. "Slip into that pajama top and come to bed."

I folded up my uniform and spent quite some time arranging it carefully on the dresser. When I finally moved toward the bed, she held the covers open and slid over to make room for me.

Nothing happened at first, but after we'd lain there and talked for a while I quit shaking and my body began to respond and we made love and it took about fifteen seconds. I said I was sorry I had let her down by finishing so fast, but she said she'd been waiting for this exact moment for three years and it was wonderful. It was an awfully nice thing for her to say.

CHAPTER 11
LOOKING FOR A JOB

A few days later I drove the farm truck into town. I wore a pair of new overalls and shitkicker shoes. No uniform, no ribbons. I parked in front of the courthouse and went into Dad's office. Jess was sitting there by himself, sucking on a kitchen match.

"Much obliged for clearing everybody out of the house the other day," I said.

He gave me a big thumbs-up sign. "Well, I know what I would've been thinking about if I was gone for three years."

I thought I'd experiment with a little brotherly teasing, so I said, "If you're still the way you used to be, I know what you would've been thinking about if you were gone for three *hours*."

He was pleased at the compliment to his manliness. "I reckon that's about right," he said modestly.

"Irene wrote me you married a girl from Fredonia."

Jess leaned back in his chair and put his feet up on Dad's desk. He was wearing a pair of brown cowboy boots with fancy stitching. "Yeah, Mary Ruth Gilcrease. Her dad owns that Hereford farm up there between Fredonia and Princeton. Big old mansion with the white pillars. He helped me and her buy a nice house out on Moore Hill, overlooking the highway."

I felt a little burst of envy. "Sounds like you're doing all right."

"Not bad. I've got some irons in the fire."

"Like what? I've got to find something to do for a living."

"Oh, Dad'll find you something, but you need to learn to play the game."

"What game would that be?"

"The politics game, the game that's kept Dad in office for a quarter of a century, *that's* what game." It seemed to me like he was trying to tell me something without coming right out and saying it.

"What's Dad got going now besides the funeral home?"

"Let's see, there's the flour mill, and the hardware store, and some other investments."

What other investments? "What's the deal on the hardware store?"

"He bought the store from Old Man Jick Fuson after you went overseas. It's over there on South Street, you know, and Dad bought the vacant lot next to it and started a big lumber yard. It'll be a gold mine with this building boom that's going on."

Could I clerk in a hardware store? "Do you reckon I could work over there?"

"Maybe, but I think Dad's kind of got that business earmarked for me. I won't always be a deputy sheriff." Jess had a crafty look about him, a man on the make.

"Well, I can tell you I'm not about to work in the funeral home. I've seen enough dead people to last me a while."

"I think Hack's being set up over there, anyway, as soon as he can go to undertaker school."

I was beginning to get the picture. There was a master plan, but I didn't seem to be fitting into it too well. I swallowed my pride and said, "What do you reckon he's got in mind for me?"

"He wants you to just be a deputy for a while and be visible and let folks feel good about treating you like a war hero. Hell, you won everything but the Medal of Honor and you should've got that too. Pocketful of Purple Hearts, battle scar there on your jaw. Perfect."

"But I don't want to do all that stuff!"

"Maybe not, but it's powerful stuff. Dad wants you to join the veterans' organizations, go to church, shake a bunch of hands, tell people war stories."

"I don't feel like talking about the war, and nobody'd believe most of it anyhow. *You* wouldn't believe it."

"All right, all right. We don't have to decide anything right now. What do you say we run out to my house and get a cup of coffee? I want you to meet Mary Ruth."

"Sounds good to me."

"I'll just call out there and tell her we're on the way."

Mary Ruth proved to be a nice-looking blonde woman, although she was a little tall for my taste and maybe a little bit too horse-faced. She had a great figure and a Betty Boop voice, and she acted like what she was, the only child of a rich Caldwell County farmer. She'd been a cheerleader at Murray State when Jess was on the football team, and they got married in a June wedding about the time I was busy with some rough stuff at Ste-Mère-Église.

Mary Ruth wasn't ever going to be a genius but she was a pie-cooking fool. After she handed me and Jess our coffee, she brought out two slices of the best coconut pie I ever ate. Later on, she insisted on giving me a tour of their fine home, complete with all the modern conveniences we didn't have out in the country, like indoor plumbing and electricity.

I felt out of place in my overalls. From what I saw, Mary Ruth's father must have helped her and Jess out a right smart, because there was no way Jess should have been able to afford all the nice furniture and furnishings in their house. Paintings on the walls and everything. For my part, I liked living out at the big house with Irene.

Dad was sitting at his desk when we got back to the courthouse. He probably wasn't happy I hadn't worn my uniform like he told me to, but he didn't say anything. Jess nodded in his direction and said, "I was talking to Gene about the deputy's job that's just come open."

"That's good, I was wanting to talk to him about it myself." He leaned forward and put his elbows on his desk. "Son, I want you to come to work up here. I can start you out at the same salary I could get a more experienced man for."

Apparently the conquest of Nazi Germany didn't count as experience, at least in Dad's mind. "What kind of experience would a fellow need to have for this job?"

"He'd need to have a commitment to public service, for one thing."

That sounded like horseshit to me, and before I could stop myself I said, "You mean the way a buzzard's got a commitment to a dead cow?"

He flushed and his big teeth snapped. He and I both knew his own commitment to public service hadn't stopped him from becoming a wealthy man, but you could tell he wasn't used to people talking back to him that way. He pinched his bottom lip between his thumb and forefinger and reflected on things for a minute. "I'll just let that one go by, but you'll have to straighten up if you want to work for this county. The voters won't tolerate that kind of a smart mouth. These ain't a bunch of Army recruits you'll be dealing with, you know."

"I guess I was thinking maybe I'd just work on the farm or in one of the businesses. I don't know if I've got what it takes to make the voters happy."

"You can farm up a storm if you want to, and maybe I can find something else for you later on, but right now I need you to work out of the courthouse for a while. You've got a nice little wife out there and she'll be needing some cash money to run on. She might like to have a new dress once in a while. Maybe take a little vacation."

He really knew how to get at me, so to make a long story short I knuckled under and took the job. For the first few weeks I tried to do what they wanted, but I just grunted when people asked me brilliant questions like how many Japs did I kill or was I ever on a submarine, and I'm afraid I was a little short-tempered with a carload of voters I stopped for being drunk. Fortunately, nobody needed more than a few stitches.

There were other incidents as well. Dad bore with me for a while, but he finally banished me to the night shift so my bad disposition wouldn't be quite so much of a political liability. Thus I became the night deputy, and I also worked on the farm in the daytime and slept when I could.

As I prowled the dark highways and back roads I knew that, if a problem arose, the citizens of the county wouldn't hesitate to telephone Dad at his living quarters in the Crittenden Hotel, and Dad wouldn't hesitate to get dressed and march up to the courthouse, where he'd get on the two-way radio and dispatch me to wherever he thought I needed to be. The people of Crittenden County were pretty sturdy and self-reliant and tended to handle most of their own problems, so if they went to the trouble to call for help they probably needed it.

My primary job was to handle situations that arose as a result of nighttime criminal activity. Often the wrongdoers were drunk and violent. I was usually scared of them and there was never anybody to back me up. When I got real scared, though, I also tended to get real mad, resulting in a few citizens getting themselves banged up for being scornful of authority or resisting arrest.

I might as well go on and say that since I've been in law enforcement I've never lost a fight. One might suppose I'm a big liar when I say that, since I'm admittedly chickenhearted and since I'm only about five foot seven and weigh only about one thirty-five with rocks in my pockets. But there are some secrets to my success.

First, the Good Lord gave me really quick reflexes that got tuned up even more when I was overseas. It's almost like I get some kind of omen or premonition that something's fixing to happen, and I can begin to react even before it starts happening. Good reflexes are a great help to you when you're in a tussle.

Second, I make it a practice never to hit anybody with my fist when a blackjack or a hickory nightstick will do just as well. You can sometimes end a fight real quick with one of those instruments.

Third, I never waste time jawing with some scofflaw about how things are going to be. I ask him nice one time only, and then I knock the shit out of him and take him to jail. In that kind of situation, it's important to hit him before he hits you.

Fourth, and most important, I've got an honest face and a fellow just knows I'm telling him the truth when I point an Ithaca pump shotgun at him and tell him I'm going to blow his fucking head off unless he does exactly what I say.

CHAPTER 12

IN THE
TRADEWATER BOTTOMS

I worked the night shift for a couple of months before Dad called me into his office. "Now, son, you're doing a fine job out there, and you've made some good arrests and handled yourself okay in some bad situations."

This, of course, was leading up to something. "Exactly what am I doing wrong?"

"Nothing really *wrong*, but maybe a little bit too rough for a county deputy."

"Do you want me to stop arresting people?"

"No, but I want you to ease off on the ass-whippings."

"I haven't started a single fight."

"No, and you ain't done a damn thing to avoid one either. Look, I want you to take up for yourself and protect the people of this county, but I'm asking you to try being a little nicer while you're doing it."

This little sermon came from a man who had shot his girl-friend's husband dead not thirty yards from where we were sitting.

"If it is niceness you want, it is niceness you shall have," I said, and gave him a snappy salute. Fuck him.

Later on, I sat in the patrol car alongside Highway 60 in the Tradewater River bottoms, listening to country music on WSM. A full moon lit up the countryside and the smell of honeysuckle wafted through the open windows. My supposed purpose that night was to catch speeding motorists, thereby generating a little revenue for the county, but I sure wasn't enchanted with the idea of being a traffic cop.

The car was a pre-war Ford flathead V-8 coupe, blessed with certain performance-enhancing modifications. It would run faster than I would ever want to drive it. As for me, I wore khaki work clothes, a badge, and an old brown snap-brim hat. Under the khakis my body was scarred and puckered by bullets and metal fragments that had been furnished to me free of charge by the armed forces of the late Benito Mussolini and Adolf Hitler.

I was probably better armed than most county deputies were in those days. In addition to my rifle and a county-issued shotgun in the trunk, I carried a military .45 in a belt holster, a short-barreled .38 Colt revolver in my left hip pocket, and a blackjack in my right hip pocket. Secured in a rack in the patrol car were a flashlight and a hardwood nightstick.

I was close to dozing off when I saw headlights coming toward me in a hurry, and then a new Packard flashed past going about ninety miles an hour. I made a quick U-turn and started in pursuit. The driver slowed down when he saw the red light, and he pulled over as I caught up with him.

I stopped behind him on the shoulder of the highway, checked out his license plate, and walked up to the driver's side. There was a second man in the passenger seat. "Hidy," I said. "What part of Ohio are you all from?"

"Cincinnati," the corpulent driver replied, with that barely concealed scorn a city man often has for his country cousin. "What's the problem?"

I didn't like his snotty attitude, but Dad wanted me to be a little more pleasant to people. "Have you seen the Reds play this year?"

"A couple of times."

"I was glad to see old Bucky Walters is still pitching for the Reds. Let me see your license, please sir."

The driver took his license out of his wallet and handed it out the window. "Sorry if I was going a little too fast. It's a new car and I'm not used to it."

I couldn't think of anything pleasant to say in response to that load of crap, so I stuck with baseball. "I look for the Cardinals to win the pennant now that Musial and Slaughter are back from the service," I said. "How much have you had to drink tonight?"

The expression on the driver's face reflected his annoyance at the question. "Couple of beers with my supper in Evansville. Certainly not enough to affect my driving."

"Couple of beers, you say? How fast were you going when I fell in behind you?"

"About sixty, I guess."

"Why, you're nothing but a damn liar!" I had no idea why I was suddenly so angry at the driver, who was nothing more sinister than a tubby Yankee with a fast car. I needed to get control of myself, so I took a deep breath and looked across at the passenger. "What's *your* name?" I said.

"William Van Wyck."

"Dutchman, huh?" I took more deep breaths and noticed my hands were shaking.

"My family's Dutch, yes sir."

"Are you from Cincinnati too?"

"Yes sir."

"I've known some pretty good Dutchmen. I spent a little time in Holland a couple of years back and—"

"Now hold on," interrupted the driver, with incredible stupidity. "We've got to get to Paducah for a business meeting. Isn't there some way I can just pay something directly to you so we can get on down the road?"

"Are you trying to bribe me, you son of a bitch? How'd you like me to pull you through that window and whip your ass all over this highway?" My efforts to control myself had gone by the board.

The driver ate humble pie. "I wouldn't like it, sir, I'm sorry." He didn't stop to consider that he was about twice my size, or that it would have been physically impossible for any combination of deputies, machines, or draft animals to pull him through the window of the Packard in one piece.

"Shut up!" I said. "The reason I stopped you is because of some bad curves just down the road here on Rosebud Hill, and I didn't want you to wrap your fine new car around a tree. Now get going, and drive the speed limit from now on."

Puzzled at not getting a ticket, the driver put the car in gear. "*Wait!*"

The driver took the car out of gear and waited.

I looked in the window and did my best to give those Ohio boys a crooked smile. "Drive safe and be sure and visit Crittenden County again real soon," I said. I figured Dad would approve of that bullshit remark. The men appeared bewildered as they crept away at about thirty miles an hour.

When their taillights were out of sight, I sat on the front bumper of my car and lit up a smoke. There was no traffic except for a trailer truck I could hear double-clutching its way toward me up and around the sharp curves at Rosebud Hill. I heard it begin to pick up speed as it topped out on the hill and then suddenly I could see its headlights and a flame coming from its stack as it hit the flat stretch of highway where I was sitting. The driver was working his way up through the gears, really winding them up, and just getting up a good head of steam when he spotted the patrol car parked on the shoulder of the road. He eased off on the throttle, and I could hear just the least little hiss of air from his brakes as he tried to slide past me without getting a ticket.

Lucky for him I wasn't a bit interested in stopping a truck driver trying to make up a little time in the Tradewater bottoms. I was busy feeling bad about letting myself get so pissed off at the slob from Ohio, and I was worried that Dad was right. Since I came home it seemed like I had a short fuse all the time.

I didn't start out life having a bad disposition. Before the war, everybody thought I was easygoing to the point of being a sissy and a mama's boy. Dad himself used to make fun of me for it. I remember being at the courthouse one time when he was amusing a gang of his courthouse cronies by telling them what a weak sister I was. "Why, old Gene wouldn't say shit if he had a mouthful, would you, Gene?" he said, and everybody had a good laugh about that. There was nothing I liked better back then than being mocked by a bunch of slack-jawed courthouse loafers.

So I resolved to work hard on being a little more of a sunbeam when dealing with the public.

CHAPTER 13

BIG NILLY

Dad called me at a few minutes past noon one Sunday, while Mom and Irene were still at church. I was still in the bed from working all night and I had to jump up and run for the phone when I heard it was our ring on the party line. I wasn't happy at being disturbed, so I snatched the earpiece off its hook and said, "Speak!"

"Gene?"

"Oh, hey Dad."

"Hey son, listen, I need a big favor."

This kind of soapy talk wasn't Dad's style, so I was immediately on my guard. "Go ahead."

"Have you by chance heard of a woman name of Manilla, M-A-N-I-L-L-A, Greavis, G-R-E-A-V-I-S? Manilla B. Greavis, to be exact."

"Doesn't ring a bell."

"Well, she lives out on the Bee Creek Road, and she's been known to . . . uh. . . let men use her for money."

"You mean she's a whore?"

"A soiled dove or fallen woman is more how I'd phrase it."

"Since when? Is there somebody there with you?"

"Why yes, as a matter of fact, I'm up here at the courthouse with some ladies from two or three of the better churches here in town. They're standing here with me now. They've been kind enough to direct my attention to this matter of public concern, and I shore appreciate them taking an interest the way they done."

"This whore you're talking about, she wouldn't be the one they call Big Nilly, would she?"

"I believe that is the very person we've been speaking of."

"So what do you want me to do?"

"It's been reported by the rural mail carrier that there's two little boys living there, and I need you to ride over and check on their welfare. You know, health and morals and so forth."

"Sure, I can do that."

"Great, great. Why don't you go in to work early, then, since this is a matter of grave importance to the voters of this county?"

"You mean like now?"

"Exactly, perfect. Thanks, son, I'll ring you up a little later. Bye now."

The phone rang again in about ten minutes, and you could tell from the way he was talking that the church ladies were no longer listening to what he was saying. "Gene, Nilly Greavis is a whore, both at law and in fact, and always has been. She's probably been at it twenty-five or thirty years."

"Getting pretty old for a whore, then?"

"Age don't plug up no holes, son. Wasn't you ever over there to see her when you was a boy?"

"No."

"Oh." He sounded like I'd let him down by my failure to get my ashes hauled by a lewd woman. Yet another disappointment for him.

"All right, what is it you *really* want me to do?"

"Put your uniform on and drive over there. Tell her you're there to check on them little boys, and if they're okay—not black and blue or starving, you know—just tell her to behave herself as long as they're there. Probably grandkids or something."

"I've never laid eyes on her. What does she look like?"

"Big handsome woman when she was younger, roan-colored hair and all, but she's put on considerable flesh. Named after Admiral Dewey's battle—Manilla Bay, you know—so that'd make her a few years younger than your mom, wouldn't it? Got a mean streak a mile wide if you make her mad, so watch out."

"I think they spell *Manila* with only one *L*, don't they?"

"She spells it with two, but I know a smart boy like you can straighten her out. When you get out to her house, make damn sure you tell her right off the bat that she don't know how to spell her own name. She'll get a kick out of that! Now get cracking, and call me as soon as you get back, so I can report your findings to them women on the church vigilance committee."

I hung up without further comment because I knew Dad hadn't intended to pass a compliment when he called me a smart boy. Just the opposite, in fact. Typical of him to ask me for a favor and then insult me in the same breath.

Irene and Mom came home from church about that time, so I ate a leisurely Sunday dinner with them before I put on my uniform and headed for the Bee Creek Road. I knew where the hillbilly whore lived. I had actually been over there to her place with a couple of my friends when I was in high school, but I stayed in the car when they went inside. I was so scared and guilty feeling I didn't think I could do anything with her if I *had* gone in and, anyway, I was already planning to marry Irene at the time.

When I pulled up to the house I could see it was pretty dilapidated. No foundation, just built on stacks of flat sandstone rocks. Behind the house were some sorry-looking outbuildings, but I could also see a nice Holstein milk cow and a big flock of Dominicker chickens. A black and white cow, with matching black and white poultry!

There was no sign of any little boys, but there was a monster working in the well-kept garden who had to be Big Nilly. She was over six feet tall, with a great wide face and little piggy eyes. Although carrying a lot of fat on her bones, she had shoulders as wide as a fullback's and legs like tree trunks. She was wearing a sleeveless dress that was popping its buttons, and she was bare-footed. No hat or bonnet adorned her big hog head.

When I stepped out of the patrol car, she leaned on her hoe and scowled at me. Remembering my manners, I gave her a wave and said, "Good afternoon, ma'am. I'm Deputy Sheriff Eugene Taylor. Can I talk to you for a minute?"

She looked me over for a few more seconds and went back to her hoeing. I eased on over to the edge of the garden and waited till she looked at me again.

"Ma'am, I really need to talk to you about something."

She gave me a death stare and said, "I reckon you can't see I'm busy, can you?"

"I'm sorry to bother you, but it's been reported that there's a couple of children living here under inappropriate circumstances."

"Mister, you ain't taking them kids away. Them's my grandba-bies."

I'd taken about all the backtalk from this woman that I could stand. "Look, lady, the last thing I want to do is take them kids away from you, but I've got to check on their welfare and make sure they're okay. Now trot 'em out here, and be damned quick about it."

Big Nilly's little red eyes smoldered and it didn't look like her brain was processing what I was trying to tell her. "Mr. Deputy, I ain't a-gonna let you take them babies off this place."

"Goddammit, woman, I've already told you *I do not want to take them kids anywhere!* I just want to see that they're okay. It ain't that complicated!"

As a man experienced both in warfare and in civilian scuffling, I can vouch for the fact that fat people must never be underestimated. Most of the time they've got big strong legs from hauling all that blubber around and they can move awful fast for a short distance, like a rhinoceros or an elephant or something.

I suppose I shouldn't have been surprised, therefore, when Big Nilly suddenly came charging up out of the garden, but I almost couldn't comprehend that the blade of her hoe was quartering down toward the left side of my skull. I felt the wind on my face as I flung myself backwards, and I had to scramble for my life again as the hoe thunked into the ground right where I'd been the instant before. By the time I regained my feet, here she came again, and there was nothing for me to do but turn and run.

I was in a dilemma. If she'd been a man, I would've stuck a .45 ball into her little reptile brain by now, but she *wasn't* a man, was she? I know you're supposed to honor your mother and be a true loving husband to your wife, and I know you're not supposed to mistreat women, but what was I supposed to do here? While I was weighing these propositions, Big Nilly was chasing me around the house with homicide on her mind. *She* certainly wasn't experiencing any ethical problems.

As we raced back around to the front of the house I spotted an empty wooden Pepsi-Cola case laying on the porch. I grabbed it and spun around, using it as a shield. When Big Nilly swung the hoe again I parried her strike and then moved inside of her guard before she could recover. That's when she found out right quick that a hoe isn't a very good defensive weapon, for I was able to get in close to her and bust that cold-drink case over her head. Her knees buckled and her eyes rolled back and it was sleepy time at the whorehouse.

I was breathing hard by now, and it was all I could do to drag her big ass over to a shade tree and prop her up in a sitting position.

She was bleeding a little from where her head was split open. She was too much woman for a mere set of handcuffs, so I took a coil of rope out of the trunk of the patrol car and tied her securely to the tree. It took quite a bit of rope. Then I put my hands on my knees and tried to catch my breath. But the fight wasn't over.

Wham! I saw stars and felt a hell of a pain at the back of my head and then another stabbing pain down around my left shoulder blade. I thought I was shot, because I got shot several times during the war and I know what it feels like. But no, it wasn't a *Waffen-SS* patrol operating there off the Bee Creek Road, it was the "grandbabies" themselves! There were two of them, dressed in raggedy clothes, but otherwise in the pink of health. The older one looked about twelve or thirteen years old, and he and his partner were picking up more rocks to hurl in my direction.

"Knock it off!" I cried.

"Leave Gammer alone, you shitass!" Two more rocks came my way with surprising accuracy and velocity, and I was lucky to avoid being hit again.

"Damn you, stop throwing rocks or I'll shoot you with this pistol."

"Yaah, yaah, yaah," howled the boys.

I was having a bad time. In the recent past, Uncle Sam had presented me with a number of awards for alleged valor in combat, yet I'd just been chased around a house by a lard-assed woman swinging a garden implement, and now I was treed by a couple of runt criminals armed with rocks. I felt like a fool.

Despite my threat I wasn't yet inclined to shoot the youthful outlaws, so I did what any other red-blooded boy would have done under similar circumstances; I started throwing rocks back at them, hoping all the while that no squarejohn citizen would drive past and catch me doing it. The lads seemed surprised at the accuracy and velocity of *my* projectiles and they soon retreated out of range and held a council of war. After they talked for a while, the older one raised his middle finger in my direction, and then he and his accomplice sat down on the ground to await developments.

Keeping an eye on the boys, I squatted next to Big Nilly pending her return to consciousness. After a few minutes, her eyelids fluttered and then all of a sudden she was wide awake.

"You've cracked my head open, you little cigarette-dick."

I was embarrassed and mad, so I used some plain language. "Listen here, you sow, you're about this close to going to the penitentiary for attempted murder, and them so-called grandbabies of yours are even closer to being sent off to reform school. Is that what you want? Yes or no?"

The plain talk sort of got her attention and she shook her head. "No sir, that ain't what I want. I was just afeared you was about to take them boys away from me."

"No, I'm not aiming to do that, provided you're taking good care of them. I've just got to make sure they're okay."

"Well, why in the *world* didn't you tell me that in the first place, and save us all this trouble?"

"I really do wish I would've thought to tell you. I blame myself for everything that's happened."

"What all do you want to know about me taking care of them kids?" She cranked her head around so she could see the rock throwers and yelled, "You, James Edward, come on over here and talk to this deputy. You too, Frank."

The older little brute shook his head. "Gammer, he's been a-throwing rocks at us and cursing."

"Shut your lying little mouth and get on over here. This man's a deputy sheriff and he ain't lowdown enough to throw rocks at innocent childern. Do I look like a idiot to you?"

James Edward and Frank didn't answer their grandmother's question, which was just as well. They looked at me through slitted eyes and crept over toward us, ready to bolt at any sign of renewed hostilities. When they got close, I said, "Which one of you all is the smartest?" but they wouldn't answer that question either. "All right, fine . . . James Edward, what did you all have for breakfast this morning?"

James Edward was surly. "Scrambled eggs and fried squirrels and coffee."

"It's not squirrel season, so where did you all get the squirrels?"

James Edward jerked a grubby thumb in his sidekick's direction. "Shank here accidentally hit 'em with a rock."

"I never done any such a thing!" shrilled young Frank, who appeared to be a bit foolish. "You done it yourself, and it weren't no accident!"

"Okay, forget it, forget it," I said to the outraged little dimwit. "But . . . say, is your name *Frank* or is it *Shank*?"

"It's *Shank*, cause I can't pernounce *Frank*."

"But you just now said *Frank*, didn't you?"

"No I never . . . I said *Shank*!"

Clearly, it was time for me to move my investigation along. "Well, *Shank*—for God's sake, wipe your nose, boy—where's your mama at anyhow?

The little dullard smeared at his nose with the back of his hand. "She went off in a red car with an old man that owns a bunch of grocery stores."

"Well, where's she at now?"

"Don't know, don't care."

"When's she coming back?"

"Be back this fall sometime, she said. Me and James Edward don't care whether she comes back or not. We like living with Gammer."

I turned back to James Edward, who appeared resentful at being left out of the proceedings. "Have you all had your Sunday dinner yet?"

"Yeah."

"Who fixed it?"

"Gammer."

"Was it fit to eat?"

"Yeah."

"What all did you have?"

"Baked chickens and boiled taters and green beans and milk and fried pies. Gammer et one chicken and me and Shank et the other one."

"You all look like the kind of boys that'd need a lot of whippings. Is that about right?"

There was a long pause while James Edward rolled his eyes back in his head and considered how best to respond. Finally, he committed himself: "Maybe."

"What does your Gammer use on you when she whips you?"

"A peach tree switch. She makes us go break it off the tree ourself."

"All right, you all go on about your business. I'm fixing to untie her so she and I can have a little talk, and then I'll be leaving."

Big Nilly said, "You all go find your fishing poles and see if you can catch us a mess of fish for supper." In spite of her rough talk she seemed to have a real affection for dear little James Edward and Frank—future felons though they might be.

After I untied her and helped her up, we went and sat on the porch. The splintered Pepsi case lay nearby. "You're a pretty tough little man," she said. "Whose boy are you, anyway?"

"Mrs. Lera Taylor's my mom and Sheriff Ross Taylor's my dad."

"You're old Man o' War's son, are you?"

"I reckon that's right, if that's what you call my dad."

"That's what I used to call him but it wadn't cause he could run fast, if you take my meaning. You don't look nothing like him."

"How do you happen to know my father, Miss Manilla?"

"Why, he come to see me for years, one of my first customers when I become a sporting girl. Long before you was born, I expect. After he got elected the first time, I never even charged him when he come a-courting. But then I got older and fatter and he quit wanting any of this thing, so he told me I had to start paying him a little cash once in a while for my license to operate. Of course it wadn't what you'd call a real paper license."

"But you never got arrested, did you?"

Big Nilly made no verbal response, but she leaned to one side and passed gas loudly. "*Another cabbage head busted,*" she cried, pleased with herself. "How come you never did come to see old Big Nilly like Jess and Hack done?"

"Jess and Hack both?" I couldn't believe it.

"Not at the same time, but I broke 'em both in, all right. A growing boy's got to have his vitamins, and they got their first taste of Vitamin P from me. They're better men for it, but I can't figure out how I missed out on you."

"My loss, I reckon."

"Tell you what, while them kids is down on the creek bank, why don't you and me step in the house and I'll show you what you missed out on. No charge."

"Much obliged, but I'm a married man."

"Well, like you say, it's your loss. Your wife'd thank you for what I could learn you about some things. Wouldn't take ten minutes."

"No ma'am, I don't believe she'd appreciate it at all. Now listen to me, you take good care of them boys. Keep putting good food on the table and don't whip them with anything bigger than a switch, and don't be whoring when they're around to walk in on you. You do all that and me and you won't have any more trouble."

"You got a deal, little feller. Say hello to old Man o' War and tell him it wouldn't kill him to stop by once in a while for old time's sake."

CHAPTER 14

THE PREACHER IN
THE HAYFIELD

From the kitchen porch of the big house, one looks out across the calf pasture toward the fields on either side of the Blackburn Church Road. The road runs due south for a little over half a mile from its intersection with the Porter Mill Road, and then curves sharply to the east for about five hundred yards to the old Coop sawmill place, then south again across the Big Piney bridge, past Blackburn Church and Cortez McDowell's farm, and eventually on to Shady Grove. The long north-south stretch of road is what we call the Long Lane. It's where the fast racking horse Ruby Laffoon bucked Dad off that time, to the everlasting amusement of Mr. John Lloyd Pruitt.

One blazing hot day, not long after my run-in with Big Nilly Greavis, I was mowing hay in the big fields on the west side of the road. I wore overalls, a blue chambray work shirt, and a straw hat, and I sneezed over and over with great violence. I was driving our new rubber-tired tractor hitched to a sickle-bar mowing machine, and I'd just finished setting a land speed record for a B Model John Deere after I ran over a yellowjackets' nest.

The two-cylinder engine pop-popped as I headed toward a gap that led into the next field. As I drove through the gap I saw Shad Westmoreland, one of our hired men, coming into the field I'd just finished mowing. He was aboard the old spoke-wheeled John Deere, pulling a hay rake. We were planning to bale hay tomorrow or the next day if it didn't rain.

I stopped and ran back to warn Shad about the yellowjackets and then I started clockwise around the outside of the unmowed field. Grasshoppers whizzed back and forth around the tractor and I could see some buzzards wheeling high above the creek bottoms off to the southwest toward Riffle Hill. A dead cow, maybe, but too far away to be one of ours. When I came to the end of the long side of the field, I locked the brake on the right rear wheel and turned the front wheels sharply to the right, squaring off my corner. Then I was off again along the short side of the field.

The sun was already high up in the hazy white sky and I began to think of my noon meal, which was even then being prepared by Mom and Irene at the big house. I hadn't gotten much sleep after working the night shift, so I'd only taken time to wolf down a bowl of corn flakes before hurrying to help with the morning chores and then on to the hayfields.

After making a few circuits around the field, I stopped to have a drink from my water jug and became aware of a man approaching me on foot. He wore dress pants and a white shirt with a tie loosened at the collar. He'd parked his car on the side of the road and straddled the barbed wire fence to come into the hayfield. I looked at him sourly and sat on the tractor with the engine idling.

When the man got closer, he said, "Hot enough for you?"

"Just about right," I said.

"I'm Brother Draper from the Sunshine Methodist Church. I was talking to your father about you the other day, and I thought I'd come out and invite you to come to church with us on Sunday."

"You and my father, huh? That's quite a combination, but I reckon I'll pass on the church services."

"Well we'd sure love to have you."

This guy was getting on my nerves real fast, but I was actually trying hard not to be rude. I just wanted him to go away so I could get on with my work. "My religion sort of got readjusted when I was overseas."

"You were in the Army, weren't you?"

"That's right."

"Combat?"

"Yep."

He wasn't doing much good in the conversation department, so he started off in another direction. "Did you study the Bible when you were growing up?"

"Yeah, my mom took us to church at Blackburn Baptist, just around the road yonder. But a Methodist told me one time that Baptists aren't as smart as Methodists are. Do you reckon that's true?"

"I know plenty of smart Baptists. What was your favorite Bible story?"

I thought about it. "I'd have to say it's the one where the old gent got a couple of she-bears to eat up forty-two head of children for making fun of his bald spot."

"That was Elisha, who was impatient with little children. Myself, I tend to favor the teachings of Jesus: *Suffer the little children and forbid them not.*"

"Well, I imagine Elisha did a lot better job of making the kids mind their parents and say please and thank you."

"Maybe so," the preacher said. "But, let's face it, I'm in the New Testament business."

During this conversation he was so pleasant and good-humored without being a sissy that I began to feel guilty about messing with him, so I said, "They tell me preachers are always hungry.

Why don't you come on up to the house and eat dinner. It's almost noon, so it'll be ready when we get there."

"That'd be wonderful," he said, just a little too quickly for anybody but a Methodist parson hungry for pie and cake. "I'll drive us up there and bring you back later on."

That evening after supper, Irene and I sat on the front porch of the big house, outside the door that opened into our bedroom. Old Whitey lay nearby, thumping his tail on the floor of the porch whenever he thought anybody was paying attention to him. Irene had kicked her shoes off and pulled her cotton dress up to the middle of her thighs to cool off. She had pretty legs and feet.

"I liked that preacher you brought up here for dinner today," she said, poking me in the leg with her foot.

"He had a good appetite, all right."

"I think there was more to him than just a mouth and a belly. He seemed like he had some walking-around sense."

"I reckon."

"And he told us he was a chaplain during the war."

"Right."

"Chaplains were in battles, weren't they?"

"Some were. Chaplain Woodall hit the silk with us on every one of our combat jumps, and Father Matt only missed the last one because he got his back boogered up when he landed in a tree in Normandy."

"Was Father Matt a Catholic?"

"Right. Donnelly was his name."

"I've never been around any Catholics that I know of."

"Well, I can tell you that the ones I knew would take a drink of liquor if it was offered."

"You could talk to a preacher like those guys if you needed to, couldn't you?"

"What would I want to talk about?" I didn't like where this conversation was going.

"Oh, I don't know. Anything you wanted to talk about, I guess." She got up and stood behind my chair and began to rub my neck and the back of my head.

"There's nothing I want to talk about, and if there was, I'd talk to you about it."

"I know you would, but I think you might need to talk to somebody who's been through some of the same stuff you have."

I didn't say anything, and after a while she said, "Would you be interested in talking to Brother Draper about the war?"

"No."

"It wouldn't be like going to a doctor or anything. I just want you to feel better, and maybe you wouldn't have so many bad dreams."

I sidestepped. "He said he was in the Navy, didn't he? He probably spent the war preaching to drunk sailors and jarheads in San Diego."

"But we don't know that for sure, do we?"

"No."

"Well, will you talk to him?"

"I'll think about it."

"When?"

"I said I'd think about it."

She went into the house, and I sat listening to the tree frogs and watching the lightning bugs in the gathering darkness. After a while, I went inside too.

If I had to come up with one word to describe my wife, that word would be "solid." She could do the work of two men with her powerful little hands, yet she was always even-tempered and cheerful like her mother. When she was helping out in the hayfield, she could snatch a heavy bale off the ground and put it up over her head onto the haywagon all in one smooth move. (Myself, I had to heist it up onto my knee before I could push it up on the wagon.) She was a pony girl, short and sturdy, and she was embarrassed that you could see the muscles in her arms and legs and back, but she was all woman.

For all the mixed-up feelings I had when I came home from the war, I tried never to show my bad temper when she was around. There really wasn't much reason to, because the only time she ever nagged me was when she wanted me to do something for my own good, like talk to the preacher about things that were bothering me. The rest of the time she was good as gold.

Because she was such a peach, I had just pushed down my sex drive when I was overseas during the war. Most of the time I had plenty of other things to think about, but even in England, and on leave in Paris, and in Berlin after the war ("*Kommen Sie hier,* baby!"), I just wasn't going to cheat on Irene. For one thing, I loved her and it wouldn't have been the right thing to do, and for another, I didn't want to be a philanderer like my father.

Before my outfit ever went into combat the boys all teased me about Irene and some of the guys from up north hinted that maybe I liked boys better than girls, but after we got bloodied up in Sicily the teasing stopped. In combat, you might say I covered all the ground I was standing on, and everybody was all of a sudden either mighty respectful to me, or else they avoided my gaze and didn't say anything at all. They got to where they were real sensitive to my feelings and I sure did appreciate it.

When I got home from the war it took a while for Irene and me to get used to each other again. The truth is, I sometimes had some problems with my manhood but eventually things started working good and we tried to spend a lot of time in bed together. After I started working the night shift I'd usually have to sleep a little during the day, and she'd try to come in and lie down with me for a while.

The featherbed didn't make a lot of noise and we fixed the headboard where it wouldn't bang into the wall, but we still had to make an effort to be quiet if Mom and Hack were anywhere around. Mom was too wise to take official notice of such things, but I noticed she worked in the garden an awful lot that first spring and summer. Just a coincidence, probably.

Making love with Irene was exciting and fun. One time I didn't get home from work till eight or nine o'clock in the morning, and she came in to join me for a "nap." She turned her back to me to slip out of her clothes, and I said, "Jess was right, all those years ago."

"About what, hon?"

"He said you had a nice fanny."

She was indignant. "Oh, he did, did he?"

"Indeed he did. Said it was like a little upside-down Valentine."

She looked over her shoulder into the mirror and said, "Do you suppose he meant the shape or the color?"

"If I had to guess, I'd say it's the shape he was talking about. I hope you've never let him have an opportunity to see what color it is."

"I certainly haven't. When was it he made that ugly remark?"

"Oh, I don't know. Years ago."

"Who did he say it to?"

"Just me and Hack."

"I think it'd do Mr. Jess Taylor a world of good if I slap his jaws next time I see him."

"I'd pay good money to see it. Come on to bed."

Afterwards, we lay in bed and talked. She ran her finger along the scar that started at the back of my jaw on the left side and reached around to my chin. "So, how'd you get this one?"

"Oh, a fellow cut me with his knife. It looks worse than it was."

"It looks like it was pretty bad."

"There's always a lot of blood with a face wound, but if you can, you just get it sewed up and keep going."

"Where were you when that happened?"

"Up in Belgium somewhere. There was snow on the ground."

"I bet I was praying for you right then, right when it happened."

"Well, I thank you for your prayer because I needed all the help I could get."

I didn't tell her, but I dreamed about that knife-wielding German soldier every couple of weeks. I still had his *Soldbuch* with his name and photograph on it, but I never showed it to anybody. His name was Hans-Dieter Kraus, *geb. am 31.7.1927 in Bremen; Religion, r.kath; Stand, Beruf, Schüler,* which means he was a Catholic boy from Bremen who was a student before he was in the army, and he was just seventeen years old when I wrung the life out of him in that cold Belgian forest. He was just one of many, but he's the one I couldn't get out of my head.

CHAPTER 15

JANUARY 1947: THE ICE BARK

The day began with snow and sleet, a cold north wind, and temperatures in the high twenties. Shortly before midday, the snow turned into a steady freezing rain that caused an icy glaze to build up on the trees and bushes. Country people called this phenomenon an ice bark. In the late afternoon, the temperature began to drop, and before long the country roads were so slick I didn't even try to get the patrol car out of the driveway for the night shift. I figured there wouldn't be many evildoers out on a night like this anyhow.

By bedtime, the thermometer on the front porch showed thirteen degrees above zero and more snow was falling on the frozen hills and fields. Right before jumping into bed with Irene I put a big hickory log into the bedroom fireplace and covered it with ashes so there'd be a nice bed of hot coals in the fireplace when it was time to get up.

Next morning, Irene had already fled to the warm kitchen when I woke up suddenly from another scary dream. I got out of bed and coldfooted my way over to the fireplace. I stirred the hot coals and threw some corncobs on top for kindling, followed by several sticks of firewood. I blew on the fire till it burst into flame and began to give off some feeble heat. Shivering, I pulled aside the window curtains and saw that several more inches of snow had fallen on top of the ice during the night. I had a pure hatred for snow and ice.

I dressed quickly and I hurried into the kitchen, made pleasant by the presence of both a Warm Morning heating stove and a wood-fired cooking range. Mom and Irene were putting breakfast on the table, so I sat down and added sugar and cream to the cup of coffee Irene set in front of me. When they joined me at the table, Mom folded her hands and waited.

I inclined my head slightly and said, "*Lord, we thank Thee for these and all Thy blessings. Amen.*"

"Amen," Mom said, "And we're thankful Haskell's already safe and sound back at school." Hack had gotten bored with Crittenden County and left to go back to Cincinnati on the day after Christmas. He was attending the School of Embalming up there and expected to be a full-fledged licensed undertaker by springtime, so he could take over operations at the Taylor Funeral Home.

As we ate, Mom said, "Eugene, you've been saying that same little blessing since you were six years old. Why don't you learn one that's a little more grown up?"

"I learned one over at Bragg that'd be perfect."

"How does it go?"

I folded my hands and bowed my head reverently. "*Rub-a-dub-dub, thanks for the grub. Amen.*"

Irene laughed and quickly covered her mouth with her napkin. Mom reached across the table and smacked me none too gently on the side of the head. "That may do nicely for a bunch of rough soldiers, but not at my table, thank you."

My beautiful wife bailed me out by changing the subject. "You know, we need to check on Shad and Shack and make sure they're okay."

I was ready to talk about something else too. "If anybody can take care of themselves it's them, but I expect we better try to call them after we eat. I hope the phone lines aren't down from all the ice."

As it turned out, the telephone lines were still intact, and Irene was able to check on Shad and Shack by the simple process of going to the wall telephone and cranking out two long rings and one short ring, their number on the party line. Shad answered the phone and told her he and Shack were fine and they had plenty of food and firewood. If they needed anything they'd telephone or, if necessary, start up the old tractor and ride it up the Long Lane to the big house. Its cleated steel wheels should have no trouble biting through the ice and snow.

That left Bob Martin. Since he didn't have a telephone, an investigation into his welfare would have to wait till the morning chores were finished. With this in mind, we scraped the breakfast dishes and threw the food scraps into the slop bucket for the hogs. Then we all put on overshoes or rubber boots and set out to take care of our agricultural empire.

One of my duties on this day was to slop the hogs and give them ears of field corn from the crib located in the barn. Next, I took a hatchet and broke the ice in the small pond out in the hog lot. By the time I'd fed and watered the mules, my nose was running and my feet felt like they were frozen solid. Eventually I found Mom and Irene and helped them finish up their work, and then we headed back to the house. Once inside we poured more coffee and pulled kitchen chairs up close to the stove to thaw out.

I was worrying about Bob Martin. "I guess I ought to go see about Bob, but I sure do hate to walk up there in this mess. I wish I had me a Jeep with some tire chains."

I think Mom was still a little put out by my paratrooper blessing. She said, "If wishes were horses, beggars would ride."

She could be mighty irritating with her proverbs and famous quotations, but this time she gave me an idea. I put on my warm clothes and my overshoes and went back down to the mule barn, where I took a bridle from the tack room and carried it to Belle's stall. She and Kate were getting on up in years and they didn't have much work to do since we got the new John Deere, so I saw no reason why she shouldn't be glad to carry me to Bob's cabin and back. She shook her head when I put the cold bit in her mouth, but after that she followed along like a lamb as I led her back up to the house. I didn't bother to put a saddle on her.

Tying her to one of the posts on the kitchen porch, I went through the house and got my rifle and slung it across my back.

"Why are you taking that?" Irene wanted to know.

I didn't really know why and it annoyed me to be asked, but I swallowed hard and said, "Oh, you never know what you might run into in the woods between here and Bob's." For some reason I felt anxious and I just thought I'd be more comfortable having a rifle with me when I rode out through the ice and snow. I pulled on a pair of brown jersey gloves and turned to leave. "I won't be gone long," I said.

I walked back outside and down the steps and I pushed against Belle's off side till she was standing right next to the porch. Then I went back up on the porch, climbed over onto her back, and rode her past the mailbox and into the frozen road.

She snorted as she started down the first steep hill on the way to Bob's, and I could see her breath in the frigid air. I felt her slip once or twice on the icy grade, but I held her in the middle of the road so the caulks on her iron shoes could maybe get traction in the gravel. Her flanks were warm on the insides of my legs.

As we got to the bottom of the hill and started slantwise up the side of the next ridge, I was all of a sudden scared nearly out of my wits by a loud report like a gunshot, followed by a large tree limb crashing to the ground just a few feet away. It was nothing more than an ice-laden limb breaking off a locust tree, but for an instant it called to mind mortar shells bursting among the trees in a far-away forest. "God *damn* it!" I gasped, recovering my composure.

As I steered Belle into Bob's yard, I was struck by the fact that there was no smoke coming from the chimney. *Why in the world wouldn't Bob have a fire going?* I rode around the cabin and called out, "Ho, Bob." No answer.

I saw two sets of footprints leading from the front door off through the woods to the southeast. On closer examination, I could tell that one set of tracks led away from the cabin and the other came back toward the cabin. It looked like both sets had been made by the same person. Then I noticed frozen drops of blood near the inbound set of tracks.

I slid to the ground, keeping Belle between myself and the cabin. I levered a cartridge into the chamber of the rifle, leaving the safety off, and I pulled off my right glove with my teeth and stuffed it in my coat pocket. After a quick look at the surrounding woods, I took hold of Belle's bridle and led her quickly toward the corner of the cabin. Keeping my eyes on the door and on the window beside it, I wrapped the reins around a little redbud tree and then moved along the front outside wall of the cabin and ducked underneath the window.

I was worried and scared and excited. I turned the knob and pushed the door open, stepping back along the wall away from the open doorway. "Bob, are you in there?" I yelled. I could hear the wind in a nearby grove of cedars and then from the cabin came a faint groan. I went through the door quickly, rifle at the ready.

Bob was in the bed with his bloody hair stuck to the ticking of his pillow. He'd piled all of his bedclothes on top of himself trying to stay warm. When I bent over to see if he was conscious I could smell whiskey breath, but there was no bottle or jar of whiskey to be found anywhere. His eyes were swollen nearly shut and his lips were split open. There was a bad gash on his head and his face was puffed up and caked with dried blood.

"Bob, who did this to you?"

He peered up at me and opened his mouth to speak, but then he closed it again and shook his head. "Better not say," he croaked.

I felt a lump in my throat, for I loved that old man. I went outside and scouted around some more, then carried in several armloads of wood and built up the fire. I drew a bucket of water from the well in the front yard and brought it back inside. I poured some in a pan and put it right in front of the fire to warm it up. When it was lukewarm I soaked a rag in it and wrung it out and used the rag with some lye soap to clean up his face the best I could. I took my pocketknife and cut the bloody hanks of his hair that were stuck to the pillow, and I put my arm under his bony old back and lifted him up so he could drink some of the warm water.

When he had drunk all the water he wanted, I said, "We've got to get you into town to a doctor, and I'll be damned if I know exactly how to do it. Do you reckon you could stay up on old Belle till we could get you back to the big house?"

He just grunted, which I took to be an affirmative answer.

Slinging my rifle again, I helped him sit up on the edge of the bed. He winced as I helped him on with his coat, and I wondered if he had any internal injuries. He put his arm around my shoulder and we eased out into the yard and over to where Belle was tied. She was a big old mule, and it was quite a struggle to get him up on her back.

I was afraid the cold would be too much for him so I went back in the cabin and got a quilt. When I handed it up to him, Belle all of a sudden got spooky and shied away and I thought he was going over the side. "Whoa up there, you bitch," I cried, and I got hold of the reins and led her into a fast walk back around the icy road toward home. I kept her in the tracks she'd made earlier, and that appeared to help her keep her footing. She seemed ashamed of herself and didn't give me any further trouble, while Bob—silent as death—slumped forward on her back and managed to keep his seat.

When I lugged Bob through the front door of the big house I went right on through the living room and back to the middle bedroom where I laid him down on one of the featherbeds, unlaced his shoes, and covered him up. Irene and Mom came in big-eyed from the kitchen, and I said, "Somebody has worked Bob over, and he needs a doctor. I turned to Irene and said, "Would you please go up in the attic and bring down the feather tick off the little bed and all the old bed quilts you can find?"

I went to the telephone and cranked the Westmorelands' number. "Shack, this is Gene. Bob's been hurt and I need for you all to help get him into town. Hitch the tractor to the road wagon and you and Shad come on up here. Dress warm. I need you to leave there as soon as you can. If there's a problem, call me back. Otherwise, I want to see you all here in the next half hour."

Only after I hung up did I stop to think that Shad and Shack were as old as Dad, and that I might have been out of line to boss them the way I did. They never said anything about it though, either then or later. It was almost like I was back in the Army: something needed to be done, it needed to be done right, it needed to be done now, and it was up to me to get it done.

I rang for the central telephone operator and asked her to connect me with Dad's private line at the Crittenden Hotel. There was no answer, so I had her ring the front desk to see if he was loafing in the lobby or dining room.

"What is it, Gene?" He knew I wouldn't be calling him just to pass the time of day.

"I just rode old Belle around the road to see about Bob and I found him nearly beat to death, so I brought him back up here."

"How bad is he hurt?"

"I don't know. His face is all bruised and bloody. I can't tell if he's hurt inside or not."

"Any idea who done it?"

"No, but his tracks in the snow make me think he'd been over toward Riley Springs somewhere. Listen, Shad and Shack are on their way up here with the old John Deere and the road wagon. We'll put Bob on a bed tick and cover him up with quilts and a tarp. Shad or Shack can drive the tractor and I guess Irene can ride in the wagon with Bob. Once they're on their way, I'll look into who did this to him."

"Oh . . . uh . . . well, you don't need to be messing around over there in that rough country by yourself. Why don't you just wait till the weather breaks, and I'll make some inquiries?"

"Inquiries, my ass! We'll have justice this very day if it harelips the governor."

"Son, listen, I'd really rather you'd leave this problem to me, since you've got no backup. I promise you I'll handle it."

"I handle problems every night with no backup, and it never bothered you before! Is there something over in there you don't want me to find?"

"No, no, of course not," he said, yammering on with more questions and suggestions, but I was tired of jawing and I hung up on him and went back out on the porch. I climbed on Belle's back again and rode her down to the mule barn, where I put a saddle on her like I should have done in the first place. As I was tightening the girth, I heard the tractor engine popping up the hill toward the big house. By the time I got back up there, Shad and Shack were in the kitchen backed up to the Warm Morning stove.

Before leaving to come to the big house, they had wisely filled the bed of the wagon with hay. I hadn't thought of that. Now they went outside and with Irene's help they arranged the bed tick, the quilts, and a tarp on top of the hay. I threw a log chain and a couple of axes in the wagon bed in case there were tree limbs down across the road.

"Do you all think you can stay on that slick road between here and the highway?"

"The cleats on the back wheels ought to cut right through to solid ground," Shad said, "but I'm worried about them steel front wheels sliding ever whichaway on the ice."

Shack opened the stove door and spat into the fire. "I'll ride in the wagon with the old man and drive the tractor if Shad ain't man enough."

Irene said, "I'll just ride in the wagon too, and make sure Bob gets admitted to the hospital okay." She turned to me. "You can come in and get me as soon as the roads clear up a little bit. I'll get a room at the hotel if I need to."

"Sounds like a good plan," I said. "Let's go tell Bob he's going on a hayride."

CHAPTER 16

LITTLE CHOLLY AND BIG MONKEY

I t was about one o'clock in the afternoon when I began following the tracks leading out from the cabin. The inbound footprints showed where Bob had staggered and fallen several times on his way back to the safety of his home. He was a tough old man or he would never have made it. I ground my teeth with rage and urged Belle along the base of the Riley Bluffs to Riley Springs where I came upon the apparent destination of the outbound tracks—a whiskey still and several barrels of frozen mash.

The snow was churned up next to the still, clear evidence of a recent struggle. On the ground, I found more frozen blood and an empty snap coin purse I recognized as belonging to Bob. Nearby was a broken gallon jar that had once contained moonshine whiskey. I figured this was where Bob got his whiskey breath.

I began casting about for the tracks of the person who had beaten Bob and apparently robbed him. I wasn't long in finding two sets of tracks, one inbound to the still and one outbound from the still off to the northeast toward the Big Piney bottoms. The footprints were huge and I knew exactly whose they were.

"Little Cholly," I muttered to myself. "What a surprise."

Little Cholly's real name was Charles Green, younger brother to Montgomery "Big Monkey" Green, and son of Miss Nannie Green and the late unlamented Roscoe Green. Miss Nannie and Roscoe always called their boys Little Cholly and Big Monkey— even though Little Cholly was a big rough bruiser just like Big Monkey—and the people who lived in our part of the county eventually began doing the same.

The deceased head of the family, Roscoe Green, had been a piss-in-the-corner ruffian—quick to use whip and fist on his animals and his family. One night about ten or twelve years ago, he fell to his death off the Riley Bluffs while coon hunting with his boys. He was drunk at the time, of course, but there was a persistent rumor that Little Cholly or Big Monkey—fed up with his meanness—may have given him a helpful nudge over the edge.

The surviving Greens reminded some people of Ma Barker and her brood, but they just weren't as cunning or as deadly as those famous outlaws from the previous decade. They were dangerous, all right, but in a chickenshit sort of way.

Little Cholly and Big Monkey were bullyboys and small-time sneak thieves, and their crone of a mother took up for them and claimed they were being railroaded whenever their sins happened to catch up with them. Big Monkey was currently sitting in the Eddyville Penitentiary for breaking his wife's arm during a drunken argument. At his trial, Miss Nannie had stated under oath that she saw the wife break her own arm in an effort to frame Big Monkey, but the jury wasn't persuaded.

Not long after Monkey's incarceration, the old woman suffered a stroke and was now confined to an old-folks' home in Marion. Little Cholly continued to live on the family farm that adjoined our property. Somebody told me he'd married a woman from Dawson Springs and moved her and her young daughter in with him.

His tracks led through the bottoms and angled up along a ridge, following a cow path down the other side to the Green farm, although there were few farming activities in evidence as I rode into the yard. "Hello, the house," I called.

He came out onto the porch wearing overalls over a suit of long johns. He wore no socks and his high-topped work shoes were untied. He was a tall, hook-nosed man, powerfully built but going to seed. He was wide and thick and slabsided. He wasn't pretty and he had no known redeeming qualities. "Get down and come in," he said.

"Oh, I can't stay. I'm just out taking a little ride in the snow." My voice was squeaky. As a boy, I was always scared of Little Cholly and I still was, but I had mayhem planned for him this time. Justice delayed was justice denied.

"Does your pappy know you're out here?"

"I don't know what he knows."

Little Cholly pretended to clean his dirty fingernails with a hawkbill knife and I could see his knuckles were skinned up. "Well, you ought to check with him before you come a-riding up on a man like this. I heard you was working for him, but I ain't seen you since you got back from the war."

"It's a shame when neighbors don't see each other. What do you hear from Big Monkey?"

"I don't never hear from him. He's over at Eddyville, you know, behind the walls."

"I expect some of them tough cons over there'll make a punk out of him if they ain't done it already. Big brave man like him, breaking a woman's arm." I was tense and ready for what was coming. I had a tight grip on my rifle, which I was fixing to use to knock Little Cholly's brains out. The reins were tied together and looped across Belle's neck, right in front of the saddle.

Cholly jumped off the porch and strode angrily over to me. He held the hawkbill in his right hand and he came so close I could smell his sour breath and see the veins in his eyes. He looked up at me and said, "You need to turn your mule around and take your little narrow ass off this property, or I'm gonna drag you down here and cut your fucking throat."

That's when I exploded. I smashed the stock of the rifle into the left side of his head and down he went into the snow like he'd been pole-axed. I wrenched the reins around and rode Belle right over the top of him and then I swung my leg across her back and landed on him with both feet, leaving him face down and gasping.

I was crying with rage now, and I began to pound him with the steel buttplate of the rifle. I avoided striking his spine because I knew I shouldn't kill him, even though I yearned to. I rolled him over and buttstroked him in the chest and belly and tried to crack a few ribs. I straddled him and held the rifle in one hand and Jap-slapped him with the other, back and forth, making sure I broke his beaky nose. I beat him till I was out of breath, and then I put the rifle across his throat and leaned down close to his bloody face. "Can you hear me, you son of a bitch?"

Little Cholly nodded, wide-eyed.

"If you mess with Bob again . . . or any of my family . . . I swear I'll come back up here and kill everything that moves . . . man, woman, dog, cat, or chicken. Do you hear me?"

Little Cholly nodded again, and he looked like he believed every word I said. There was a lot of blood on the snow.

I got up and wiped my snotty nose on my coat sleeve. I picked up Cholly's hawkbill and closed it and threw it as far as I could into a patch of sawbriars. Then I looked around for Belle, found her by the side of the house, and pulled myself up into the saddle. As I rode around past the front of the house, a woman and a peaked-looking little girl were trying to help Little Cholly up off the ground. They were shivering in their thin dresses and wailing like their hearts would break, and they shrank away from me as I rode by. It was Cholly's wife and stepdaughter.

"Well, shit," I said to myself, and I kicked Belle in the ribs to get out of earshot.

Bob got well and came home in triumph in the patrol car. Dad never mentioned anything at all about what might or might not have happened when I followed Bob's tracks back to Riley Springs. It seemed like he knew something about it, though, because he made it a point to tell me later that Little Cholly Green had moved away. I thought he was acting awfully secretive and I wondered what he was up to.

CHAPTER 17

MARCH 1947: POLICE BRUTALITY

A couple of months after my encounter with Little Cholly, I arrested two men breaking into a store down at Sheridan, a crossroads village on the Tolu Road. It was a father and his son and they'd come over from another county in the wee hours of the morning to steal and pillage. An alert neighbor spotted them and called it in. When I got down there, they had their old pickup truck pulled up to the back door of the store and they were loading up soft drinks, lunch meats, cigarettes, canned goods, and everything else they could lay their thieving hands on.

They were good-sized men, so I presented my shotgun and called on them politely to surrender and they did. I had them hug a tree and I used two sets of handcuffs to chain them to each other with the tree in between, and there they stayed while I tried to get hold of the storeowner. It took that good man a while to get there and put all his stuff back inside the store and secure the damaged rear door, but he paused in his work long enough to apply his foot vigorously to the backsides of the men who were cuffed to the tree.

Of course I wouldn't have allowed him to abuse my prisoners that way, had I known in advance that he was going to do it.

A couple of weeks later, I was in court for the examining trial to get the storebreaking case held over to the Grand Jury, and the two thieves were there, free on bond. Afterwards they followed me out of the courtroom, and I could tell from the way they were looking at me and whispering back and forth that they meant to make trouble. I went out the back door of the courthouse and started to walk across behind the Clerk's Office on my way to the patrol car I'd left parked in front of the Hole in the Wall Café on the other side of Carlisle Street. There's a little coal house in the side yard of the courthouse and that's where I stopped and turned around and lit a cigarette and waited.

The older one said, "We didn't much like the way you chained us to that there tree."

The younger one said, "We damn shore didn't, and we didn't like the way you let that man kick us in the ass, neither."

I blew a smoke ring and didn't say anything, but I was filled with dread and excitement! My heart was beating fast and there was a zippy feeling up and down my spine! I was thinking about which of the men to hit first if there was a fight. The son was bigger and probably had better endurance, but the leathery old daddy looked like you couldn't knock him down with a two-by-four. It was a hard choice, but the situation will always dictate the tactics.

The daddy said, "We think we're gonna strike some sparks off yore head."

I smiled at them and blew another smoke ring. "I'm a county officer and I want you men to go on about your business. If you come at me, somebody's fixing to be pretty God damn sorry."

The men appeared unimpressed. They glanced at each other like they were getting ready to turn their wolf loose, so I said, "Well, I *would* fight you all but I've got my new shoes on." In fact, I was wearing old shoes, but that didn't stop the two geniuses from looking down at my feet. I took that opportunity to flip my lit cigarette right up into the son's face and he let out a squall that caused me to hope I'd hit him in the eye. At the same time, I kicked the daddy hard in the groin and he groaned and went down to his knees. Then I whipped the blackjack out of my back pocket and gave myself the pleasure of knocking them both just as cold as wedges. It took about two seconds, and they still hadn't moved when I drove away.

The next day I walked into the Sheriff's Office and found Dad there telling funny stories. Jess and Mr. Blinky Coleman were gathered around him, along with a city policeman and two or three loafers. There was never a shortage of deadbeats and checker players at the courthouse.

"Anyways, there's this little old spindly country boy from over around where Piney runs into Tradewater, and he's awful jealous," Dad was saying. "So he studies about things for a while and decides he can't take it no more and he goes charging up to his girlfriend—she's a big rough Backbone Ridge gal—and he says to her, *Eye God, Sal, I'm a-getting tired of playing second fiddle.* Well, she just looks him in the eye, spits her tobacco juice, and says, *Sugarboy, with yore instro-ment, you're lucky to be in the band.*"

Everybody brayed with laughter, except Mr. Blinky Coleman, who looked like he didn't understand the vulgar punchline. He was a tangle-eyed man, and you couldn't tell what he was thinking or whether he was looking at you or at somebody else. He owned a half interest in the Marion Flour Mill and he was the operating manager. Dad owned the other half of the business and he was the silent partner. After everybody else got through laughing at Dad's joke, Mr. Coleman said, "Have you all heard anything out of them storebreakers today? Are they out of the hospital?"

"Not a peep," Dad said, "But I expect they'll be along any day with their lawyer, hollering police brutality and wanting a wheelbarrow full of money."

Jess said, "They already got exactly what they deserved."

Dad looked at Jess and then at me. "No doubt about it, but Gene should've arrested 'em for assault instead of just leaving them lay there in the courthouse yard. I've told you and told you, if you boys have got to put your hands on some son of a bitch, then you better arrest him for something."

"Do you reckon they'll sue?" Mr. Coleman asked.

"I look for their lawyer to try to twist some money out of the county by way of a settlement, but I doubt they'll sue. I reckon they could sue Gene for being a brute and they might sue me for *hiring* a brute like him, but they won't get nowhere with a jury. I mean, hell, they're just a couple of thieves and Gene's a war hero."

I was uncomfortable with the war hero stuff, but I was saved by Mr. Coleman who had a story he was dying to tell. I'd heard it many times before.

"When Gene was a little boy, he was awful softhearted," Mr. Coleman said. "One time some other kid was picking on him out at Shady Grove School, and Ross here was all embarrassed cause Gene wouldn't fight back. He thought Gene was a sissy, don't you see, and he was trying to teach him to box. The manly art of self defense, you know."

The city cop and the courthouse loafers were all ears and they nodded their empty heads to stimulate Mr. Coleman to go on with his tale. Dad was staring blankly out the window, and Jess just looked impatient and irritated.

"Anyway," continued Mr. Coleman, "I knew about the boxing lessons, so one day when Ross and Gene was at the mill I got down on my knees and pretended like I was boxing with Gene. When I finally got him to take a little weak-assed swing at me, I flopped over like I'd been hit by Gene Tunney instead of Gene Taylor. Damned if little Gene didn't just stand there and bawl, feeling sorry he'd hurt me. Ross was so disgusted he just turned around and walked out."

Jess didn't like the story any better than I did, so he said, "It's a good thing for you little Gene didn't have a blackjack with him that day, or you might've needed a few stitches in your coconut."

Mr. Coleman shrugged. "That was a long time ago. I wouldn't want to box with him now."

CHAPTER 18

MR. BURLAP AND
DOUGHBALL MCKELVEY

They wore big hats and drove a black Hudson coupe with Oklahoma tags. People thought they might be livestock buyers or mining speculators because they asked a lot of questions about local matters.

The younger one—a jolly fatboy in dark glasses—played a little snooker at the pool hall on Carlisle Street, or walked across to the square to whittle and play checkers and swap pocketknives with the courthouse regulars.

The older stranger stood about six-foot four in his pointy-toed boots, lean and hard looking—clearly not an approachable man. He would sit on a bench in the poolroom and watch his crony snooker the locals, or he might nurse a cup of coffee for half a day in the Hole-in-the-Wall Café next door. One reliable report had him lingering over a banana split at the soda fountain across from the courthouse, having a serious talk with a good-looking girl behind the counter. I didn't know it at the time, but in days to come I would hear more about the conversation in the soda fountain.

I was on my way home from court one blustery day when the black Hudson passed me in a cloud of dust and gravel. The round man was driving and the older gent regarded me sourly from the passenger seat. By the time I got to my turnoff, their car was out of sight.

The Porter Mill Road runs along a ridge, then curves to the left and down a hill to cross the one-lane bridge over Tribune Creek. As I drove down off the ridge, there in the middle of the bridge, to my surprise, sat the Hudson coupe. The chubby driver stood by the bridge rail, hawking and spitting into the creek, and the grim older fellow was standing at the rear of the car with one foot up on the rear bumper. Both were carrying modern sidearms in carved leather holsters.

I stopped my car and waited to see if the men would go on about their business. When they didn't, I got out of the car and walked up to the old guy. Before I could speak, he scowled down at me like I was some kind of a bug or reptile and said, "Son, do you know who I am?"

I was considerably put off by his arrogant manner, so I said, "No sir, are you a cowboy movie star?"

"No, you little jellybean, my name's Appling. My partner there slobbering in the creek is Mr. Doughball McKelvey."

"Are you any kin to Luke Appling the baseball player?"

"No, he's a Chicago Appling and I'm an Oklahoma Appling. My friends call me Mr. Burlap, a word play on my name, which is Burl C. Appling."

"Nice to meet you, Mr. Appling. That's certainly a clever nick-name. Now, by what authority are you and Mr. Doorknob McKelvey openly carrying deadly firearms and blocking the bridge on a pub-lic road?"

"I'm delighted you asked that question, young man. Myself, I used to work for a well-known federal agency till I got run off by the old lady in charge. She wanted sissy college boys to work for her, not some old stove-up cowboy like myself. My sidekick yon-der—by the way, he goes by *Doughball*, not *Doorknob*—he used to work for the State of Texas till he shot the wrong Mexican. Both of us was about ready for the scrap heap, but then here come the good old Treasury Department and offered us prime wages to mo-tor around the countryside pondering problems and paradoxes. We're what you might call troubleshooters."

"What kind of problems and paradoxes are you all pondering here in the middle of the Tribune bridge?"

"Well, the regular revenue men—who admittedly can't pour piss out of a boot—ain't having any luck rooting out a moonshine enterprise they think starts here in Western Kentucky and finds its way over into Southern Illinois, so me and Doughball aim to locate, and then catch or kill the people responsible. Between you and me, we think that killing 'em would be the best remedy. It saves time and money."

"Very wise."

"We're pretty sure the Illinois bootleggers are what's left of an old gang of criminal trash out of East Saint Louis who've appar-ently moved down into Little Egypt to enjoy their golden years in the Illinois country air. And *you* know all about the Kentucky end of the operation, don't you, Jellybean?"

I didn't have any idea what he was talking about, so I pretended I didn't hear his question. "What kind of a pistol is that you're car-rying, Mr. Appling?"

"It's a Colt's Model 1911, chambered in .38 Super. And I'm sure you know that Kentucky law permits me to carry it openly, even if I wasn't a federal agent."

"A pistol's a good thing to have if you need to fight your way to wherever you left your rifle."

"Yes, and how lucky I am to have several properly zeroed rifles right here in the trunk of this here automobile. I also have a Colt Monitor—that's a magazine-fed machine gun, in case you didn't know. It's got a Cutts compensator on it big as an ear of corn. Now I hate to change the subject, but me and Doughball would like you to tell us, please, about your role in the moonshine operation I mentioned. In other words, you need to stop all this fucking yap-yap and tell us what we want to know."

I really didn't know what they wanted to know, but they didn't know that I didn't know what they wanted to know. "The only moonshine I know about for sure was a one-man operation over by Riley Springs, but that fellow got saved by Jesus and moved away."

Doughball McKelvey—still fat, but no longer jolly—strolled up and said, "You're a God damn liar, you hick bastard. What if we was to shoot you full of great big holes and throw your carcass down there in the creek for the mud turtles to gnaw on?"

Burlap and Doughball clearly had me at a disadvantage, so I had to think and talk fast. "Well, see that white farm house right up yonder on the ridge. The Widow Brown sits in there all day long with a set of field glasses, birdwatching and spying on whoever's traveling this road—anything to keep her from being bored shit-less, I guess. I can feel the old hag's eagle eyes on us right now, can't you?"

Doughball took a quick peek at the house on the ridge. "I don't see no hag, and I don't feel no eyes," he said.

"Well, you better believe when my carcass lands in the creek mud, she'll be cranking her phone for the Kentucky State Police and describing two drugstore cowboys in a Hudson car who murdered Mrs. Taylor's nice boy, Eugene, in cold blood. Everybody on the party line'll be listening, so they'll hurry up and call everybody *they* know, and before you get off this road and out of the county you'll have a bunch of *hick bastards* taking potshots at your nice car. Your nifty Monitor machine gun won't do you a bit of good, either, cause you won't ever see who's firing on you. So either shoot me full of holes or get your fucking sled off this bridge so I can get on home. I'm a busy man."

"Haw, haw, haw," Doughball said. "There ain't no widder woman a-watching us, and even if she was, me and Mr. Burlap could just go up there—after we shoot you, of course—and help her remember what she seen and what she didn't see."

"Well, I'm sorry to bust your balloon, but that old woman could run both you cowpokes off with a tobacco stick. Go up there and start something with her, she'll introduce you to Old Doctor Twelve-Gauge."

Doughball turned to his partner and cried, "Mr. Burlap, this hayseed's a-trying to bamboozle us!"

Before Burlap could respond, I said, "She's buried three husbands—one got caught in a hay-baler, one fell down the well, and the last one died of belly cramps right after Sunday dinner. Some say she had a hand sending all three to the graveyard."

Doughball put his hand on his pistol. "By God, I'm gonna—"

Then Mr. Burlap did something unexpected. He burst out laughing and clapped his hands together four or five times like a grade-school teacher trying to get the kiddies to pay attention. "Boys, boys, boys, that's enough high jinks for today," he said, "though I swear I do enjoy a spirited conversation. Why, I ain't had this much fun since I kilt them three bank robbers on the Sallisaw road back in '24, but, as they say, all good things must come to an end. Me and Doughball, we've got to get on over to Bowling Green for a conference with some other revenuers, but we just wanted to hooraw you a little bit and draw your attention to our problem with that Little Egypt moonshine operation."

"Well, Mr. Burlap, I'll ponder your paradox for you while you're gone."

Doughball McKelvey still looked a little peevish. "We've done already got some suspects, *Jellybean*. By the way, you're the worst liar I ever seen, and I ain't aiming to forget it."

I raised my right hand. "Everything I've told you all is the God's honest truth, so help me."

Next day, I bought a box of chocolate candy and took it to the Widow Brown. It was the least I could do for a woman whose tough and unsavory reputation had saved my bacon. When she answered the door, she was carrying a Bible and a magnifying glass. Inviting me in, she poured us each a glass of buttermilk and we sat in her living room and talked.

"Nobody's brought me chocolates since me and my William was a-courting."

"I know you miss him, Mrs. Brown."

"Me and him was married for fifty-six years, you know, and all our kids is still living. Grandkids too, except we lost Billy in the war."

"Well, are you able to do much farming?"

"Lordy mercy, no, I just keep a cow and a few chickens and turkeys. My cataracts is so bad that about all I can do is sit in here and read the scriptures with my magnifying glass. I can still milk the cow and take care of the poultry, but I pretty much do that by feel."

"You know some people still think you're a pretty tough lady."

"Oh, go 'long home with you," she laughed. "I'm weak as a kitten and blind as a bat, but I sure do like these chocolates with caramel inside."

Not long after the Tribune bridge incident, I ran across a piece in "Life" magazine about none other than Burl C. Appling. There was a photo study of him drawing and firing his .38 Super in about two-fifths of a second. As a frame of reference, it takes me about ten times that long to present and fire my .45 out of its flap holster.

According to the article, Mr. Burlap started out as a county deputy in the Oklahoma hills, then worked as a detective in McAlester, then for the FBI, and now for the Treasury Department. Along the way, he was (by his own count) involved in about thirty gunfights and killed about seventeen or eighteen men, depending on how you counted.

Burlap was never troubled, claimed the article, if criminals got the drop on him, because he could draw and kill them before they could pull the trigger. He had in fact done this, the article said, no fewer than four times, once on the town square in Checotah, Oklahoma, once on the second floor of a hotel in McAlester, once in an alley in St. Paul, and once in the railroad yards in Mobile.

The "Life" article suggested that Mr. Burlap left the FBI following a dispute with J. Edgar Hoover over "style." Apparently, Mr. Hoover didn't like Burlap's style and vice versa. I think Mr. Hoover was the "old lady in charge" Burlap spoke about there on the Tribune bridge.

What moonshine operation were Burlap and Doughball talking about? If there was such an operation, why didn't I know anything about it? Who were the suspects Doughball mentioned? I had the feeling I was going to be in for a nasty surprise at some point in the near future.

CHAPTER 19

SEPTEMBER 1947:
DEAD IN HIS CAR

On the 18th day of September, 1947, Mom and Irene and I were at the breakfast table, talking about the incident Dad and I had been involved in the week before out at the Maude Alice Mine. There were just the three of us living at the big house now, ever since Hack moved into town and took over the management of the Taylor Funeral Home. He was now a licensed mortician, an important man in his own eyes, and he told me I must start calling him Haskell instead of Hack. I did not intend to oblige him.

The telephone rang and Irene ran to answer it. "It's Jess," she said, but as she handed me the earpiece she whispered, *"He sounds funny."*

"What's up?" I said.

"Dad's dead!" Jess's voice was hoarse.

"What?"

"He's dead, Gene."

"How?"

"In his car, out on the Crooked Creek Road by the covered bridge. He was in his car."

"Are you sure it's him?"

"It's him, all right. He was in his car."

"I understand he was in his car. Tell me what happened to him."

"I don't know. Somebody shot him or maybe he shot himself. They say his pistol was in the floorboards. You better meet me out there."

I could see the big Buick parked on a rocky outcropping that formed the north bank of the creek. He lay underneath the open car door in a pool of dark blood. His eyes were open and his socks sagged down around his white ankles. The scene reminded me of photos I had seen of Chicago gangland murders. I've seen a whole bunch of dead men but it's a jolt when it's your father, even if you didn't like him very much.

Jess was leaning against the trunk of the Buick and Hack was trying to keep the bluebottle flies away from the body. Other than that, they weren't doing anything. I got busy and scanned the area, but I found no cartridge casings, no fresh cigarette butts, no tracks on the rocky surface, no nothing.

When we moved the body, we discovered Dad had been shot once in the head at close range. There was no exit wound. In the front passenger-side floorboard I found his unfired Smith & Wesson revolver and an opened pint of Old Crow. His seersucker pants were unzipped and his suit coat and straw hat were on the back seat. His wallet held four hundred seventeen dollars in cash.

Hack shook his head like he was trying to wake up. "What in the devil was he up t-t-to out here?"

Neither Jess nor I made any response, but it was a damned good question.

There was a Cadillac hearse from the funeral home parked up on the road. At a signal from Hack, two men brought a stretcher down the embankment and we helped them wrap the body in a sheet, load it on the stretcher, and carry it up to the road. As Hack and his helpers drove away, bearing the mortal remains of Ross Taylor, Jess and I just stood and looked at each other. Then we got in our cars and headed back to town to take care of business.

The autopsy revealed what everybody already knew. My father died from the effects of a gunshot wound to the left temple, at the hands of a person or persons unknown. A deformed, small-caliber pistol bullet was removed from his brain.

As a professional courtesy, the funeral home over at Princeton prepared the body and brought it back to Marion for visitation at the Taylor Funeral Home. The Princeton undertaker did a good job, so Mom opted for an open casket. Neither the bullet wound nor any sign of the autopsy was visible.

The *Crittenden County Times* carried a long article mourning Dad's death and bragging on his many contributions to the county and to the Commonwealth of Kentucky. Sharing the front page with the story about Dad was a lively account of Marion's big win over Kuttawa in the Twin States Baseball League. Ross Taylor got murdered and Rip Wilson and Gordon Blue hit home runs.

Mom maintained a dignified and dutiful presence at the head of the casket, greeting visitors and thanking them for coming to pay their respects. She agreed with them that the Princeton undertaker did a good job on Mr. Taylor and, yes, he looked just like himself, and she urged each visitor to go to the back room and have something to eat from the mountain of food people had brought to sustain the mourners.

Irene was everywhere, greeting people she knew, finding room for flower arrangements as they came in, and making sure everybody got something good to eat. Jess's wife Mary Ruth and Irene's sisters and mom were a big help, too. My father-in-law Cortez McDowell, visibly uncomfortable in his ill-fitting Sunday suit, stood in the side yard smoking and talking to Shadrack and Meshack Westmoreland and Old Man Bob Martin.

Like Mom, my brothers and I took up our posts near the casket to greet the public. Jess was good at recognizing people, and he quietly helped Hack and me greet visitors by name. Some of them I knew already, like Miss Peggy Wilson and Miss Manilla Bay Greavis, who showed up one after the other. Each was dressed in what she conceived to be her Sunday best, and each stood over Dad and cried. I wondered whether they had anything else in common. There were other sad women as well. Some had their husbands with them and some didn't.

Toward the end of the day, Jess said to Hack, "I want you to get Mom and take her on out to the big house so she can try to get some rest. It'll be a hard day tomorrow. Don't let her give you any argument about it, either."

"Okay, Jess." Hack was happy to have somebody to tell him what to do and Jess was, after all, the new head of the family.

"Stay with her for a while and then go on home. Me and Gene will make sure everything's locked up before we leave. Most everybody's left already, anyway. Tell Mom that Gene and Irene will be along home directly."

"Right."

While Hack and Mom were leaving from the side entrance, some other visitors had come through the front door and taken a seat in the back of the viewing room. They were none other than Miss Nannie Green and her boys, Little Cholly and Big Monkey, the latter fresh from the Eddyville Pen. When I saw who it was, I was furious. The fight in the snow had been less than a year ago. Jess grabbed my elbow. "*Now, hold on,*" he whispered. "*You just take it easy.*"

The Greens had gotten up and started forward, Miss Nannie walking gimpy and lopsided because of her stroke. Big Monkey helped his mother along, keeping his eyes downcast like the well-behaved convict he was. Little Cholly looked at me and held both hands out in front of him, palms down, showing me he didn't want any trouble. I took a deep breath and waited for them to approach. I said, "Hello, Miss Nannie—Cholly—Montgomery."

"I told my boys," said Miss Nannie out of the corner of her mouth, "we better get ourselves together and go pay our respects to Mr. Taylor and his family, and both of 'em said yeah that's what we better do. My son Cholly, he come all the way from Dawson Springs." She looked me right in the eye. "He lives up there now, with his wife and her girl."

Smooth Jess said, "Why, that sure was a neighborly thing to do, Miss Nannie. Dad would've been awful proud you all came. Come on up by the casket and see him and then go on to the back and get yourselves something to eat."

"Many thanks, but we eat before we come," rumbled Big Monkey. "Mama's got the sugar diabetes and she's got to watch what she eats."

"Damn you, Monkey" snarled the old woman. "You don't have blab everything you know."

"Sorry, Mama," he said. The Greens walked up and stared into the casket and then made their way back down the aisle and out the door without saying another word or looking in my direction.

I just sat there and shook my head. It was hard to imagine being in the same room with Little Cholly without somebody getting hurt. I looked at Jess and then at my watch. "It's about time to shut down for the night, isn't it?"

"Not for a little while yet. I'm expecting a couple more people."

"Who?"

"You'll just have to wait and see. Sit down and take a load off your feet." Jess was a know-it-all and he loved to be mysterious, so I sat down and cheered myself up with a fantasy about burying the blade of a hatchet right between his eyes.

At about five minutes till six, the front door opened and a woman and a half-grown girl came in. Both were dressed in black and they headed up the aisle toward the casket. We stood up as they approached and Jess said, "Gene, you may remember Miss Lillian Blankenship. She used to work here at the funeral home when we was boys. And this here young lady's your sister, Miss April Taylor. They live in Evansville."

I was flabbergasted, but I didn't let on that I was. "I remember Miss Lillian," I said, extending my hand. I turned to the girl and surprised myself by saying, "I believe Miss April's too pretty to be our sister, but she's got a dimple in her chin that reminds me of Dad." The girl blushed and looked at the floor, and I couldn't think of anything else to say.

Jess was enjoying my reaction. "You all come on up and see him and all the nice flowers people have sent. Gene, you might go back and see if the girls have already put all the food away."

I was glad to go. When I walked into the back room, I straddled a chair and said to Irene and Mary Ruth, "Lillian Blankenship's out there."

"Who?"

"Lillian Blankenship. There was that little matter of Dad killing her husband out yonder on the street back years ago. And she's got a girl with her that Jess says is our sister. She looks it, too."

Irene was puzzled. "Your *sister*? I didn't know you had a sister."

I was ready to tear my hair out. "It's just been one damn thing after another, and now I find out I've got a woods-colt sister I never knew I had."

Irene was immediately and predictably compassionate. "Well, the poor little old girl can't help who her daddy was, can she? At least they didn't come rolling in on us while your mom was here."

"I guess this explains why Dad moved to town for good after that killing. Mom must've known about Lillian and she's had a tight jaw about it all these years. Do you reckon they're planning to come to the funeral tomorrow?"

As it turned out, Lillian and April went on back to Evansville that night. At the funeral the next day, mourners filled the church.

Brother Draper preached a thoughtful sermon, and a young man sang "If We Never Meet Again This Side of Heaven" in a fine tenor voice. I felt empty inside but not particularly sad—just the end of something familiar.

When the service was over, the funeral procession left the church and headed out West Bellville Street toward Mapleview Cemetery. The graveside service was brief and I was glad when it was over.

Jess and Hack and I all thought Dad should have been buried at Blackburn Church or at Shady Grove, but Mom insisted that burial should be at Marion. "He liked it in Marion, he lived in Marion, and he *will* be buried in Marion," she said. And that was that. She had already ordered the tombstone from the Henry & Henry Monument Company:

ROSS TAYLOR

1890-1947

"Not our will but Thine be done"

CHAPTER 20
AFTER THE FUNERAL

After we left the graveyard, Jess, Hack and I met at the Sheriff's office to talk about the murder. I brought old Bob Martin along.

Jess was upbeat. "I guess I'll be named acting sheriff till the next election," he said, enjoying the moment. "There's no reason to think I wouldn't be." He loosened his tie and undid the top button of his shirt.

"No reason at all," Hack said smugly. My brothers were political animals, but I wanted to get down to business. "What I want to know is, who killed him and why, and what do we aim to do about it?"

Jess looked at me with mild annoyance for interrupting his happy thoughts. "Well, who do *you* think it was?"

"I reckon you'd have a better idea than I would. I didn't even know till last night that I've got a bastard sister."

"Whoa!" Hack exclaimed. "Nobody told *me* nothing about a b-bastard sister. What's that all about?" He didn't look like he could take many more surprises. He was the tallest and best looking of all the Taylor men, including Dad, but it dawned on me right then that he was really kind of a weakling. He had inherited Dad's looks, but not his grit.

Jess waved off Hack's question as a matter of little importance. "Oh, back years ago, Dad was courting Lillian Blankenship. She worked here at the funeral home and he got her knocked up. Her husband took a dim view of the situation and got drunk and came after Dad, and you know the rest of the story."

"Apparently I don't know shit," Hack said.

"Oh, sure you do. After the killing, Mom made Dad move into town, remember? And he ended up giving Lillian some money so she could buy a car and move to Evansville and have the baby. He's been going up to see her and the girl ever since, and he's been giving them money every month to live on. Lillian works in a department store there in Evansville. She's really a pretty good old gal."

Hack scowled at Jess and said, "How long have you known aba-aba-about all this?"

"Since I was in high school. Why, I used to ride up to Evansville with Dad and take little April to the park while Dad and Lillian took care of whatever grownup activities they needed to take care of."

"You're a secretive son of a bitch," I said.

Jess took it as a compliment. "I do know how to keep my mouth shut."

"If you know so much, then please tell us who killed him."

Bob Martin held his hand up to be recognized and said, "I bet it was one of them Blankenships."

Jess scoffed. "There's no way one of them done it. If they meant to kill him, they'd have tried it years ago. They ain't got enough ambition to commit a murder."

"So who *was* it, Jess?"

"Well, I've been meaning to tell you, for a long time there's been a lot of, ah, untaxed whiskey moving from here to . . . uh . . . different places up north. It's possible Dad may have had some knowledge of that operation that got him killed."

"Was he trying to put a stop to it?" asked Hack.

"Not exactly, no."

The scales suddenly fell from my eyes. "He was bossing the whole operation, wasn't he?" This was the nasty surprise I had been dreading since the day I encountered Mr. Burlap and Doughball McKelvey out at the Tribune Creek bridge.

Jess compressed his lips and made no reply. He did know how to keep his mouth shut. Hack put his head down on one of the desks and appeared to tune the rest of us out.

"So who did he piss off?"

"I don't know."

"Who's hauling the whiskey?"

"The out-of-town boys send their own people to haul it."

"Who's making it? Is it the Greens?"

"They were involved for a long time, but then Big Monkey got sent to the pen and Little Cholly got religion and moved off to Dawson Springs, so I don't think they're involved anymore. It wasn't only just them, anyhow. There was a whole bunch of different little operations scattered all over the county. I think they kept moving around so the federal boys wouldn't sniff them out."

I was disgusted at all of the crookedness that had been going on behind my back, and Jess was obviously right in the big middle of it. "I say again, who did he piss off?"

"I'm telling you, I don't know. I'm looking into it. Listen, before you have a stroke, there was a tip came in a while ago that may mean something."

"I can't wait to hear it."

He looked like he was fixing to get mad, but changed his mind. "The cook at the Curve Inn Café lives out on 91 towards the Cave-in-Rock landing, but she goes home by way of the Crooked Creek Road. Anyway, on the night it happened her husband picked her up and was taking her home when they seen a car parked over there on them bench rocks where we found Dad's car. They didn't think nothing about it, because people park there all the time for drinking and romance."

"Was it Dad's car or not?"

"It must've been Dad's car, but that ain't all. About a mile past the bridge, they seen another car pulled off the road and it looked like a couple of people was in it. They thought it might've been a late model Chevy, but they didn't get a look at the license plate."

"So who do you think it was, then, a couple of out-of-town gangsters?"

"Gene, I don't know, but maybe if we find the car, we find the killer."

Bob Martin said, "I still think it was one of them damn Blankenships."

The next day, after cleaning up Dad's Buick the best I could, I found a galvanized bucket and drove out to the Crooked Creek bridge. There was still a big gout of black blood on the rocks where we found the body, so I made several trips to the creek and back with the bucket to sluice all of it away. It didn't seem right just to leave it there, but it was also hard to think about Dad's life blood all mixed up with the muddy waters of Crooked Creek.

My mind drifted back to my run-in with Burl C. Appling and Doughball McKelvey. They must have known or suspected that Dad was involved with the Little Egypt moonshine operation, and they just couldn't believe I didn't know something about it. With all the lies I told them that day, there was no reason they should give credence to anything I said.

I wondered if Mr. Burlap or Doughball may have killed Dad, but an assassination with a small-caliber pistol didn't seem to be their style. The best bet was still some racketeers from north of the river, maybe that bunch from East St. Louis that were enjoying their golden years in Little Egypt.

CHAPTER 21

LILLIAN AND APRIL

I drove to Evansville a couple of days later and found Lillian Blankenship's telephone number in the phone book. I rang her up and when she answered I said, "Is this Miss Lillian Blankenship?"

"Who's calling?"

"This is Eugene Taylor from down at Marion. I was wondering if I could come by and talk to you for a little while."

"About what?"

"About you and Dad. You know, we're trying to puzzle out who killed him."

"You don't think I had anything to do with it, do you?"

"No, ma'am."

"Well, for your information, the other night at the funeral home's the first time I've been in Crittenden County since before April was born. I wouldn't have come then except Jesse said it'd be okay. He just said we should come late in the day, and that's what we did."

"I've been wondering if maybe Dad might've said something that could point us in the right direction. I won't take up much of your time."

"Okay, I guess you can come over and eat lunch with us, but I want you to know I've heard all about you from Jesse and your

134

father, so if you say anything ugly in front of April you can just get in your car and leave."

I fought back the urge to ask her what lies Dad and Jess had told her about me. There was no telling. Finally, I said, "I won't say anything ugly, Miss Lillian. I promise I'll be a perfect gentleman."

After writing down directions to her house, I drove to a nearby grocery store where I bought a half-gallon of ice cream. Irene says you should never go visiting without taking something to your host, plus I thought I should take dessert with me if Lillian was going to feed me lunch.

Her home proved to be a neat frame house in a working-class neighborhood. It was brown with white shutters and there was an old Chevrolet coupe in the driveway. I knocked on the front door and when Lillian opened it, I held the ice cream out between her and me and said, "Thanks for letting me come over. I hope you all like strawberry."

"Thanks, it'll be fine. I was about to put the food on the table."

"Is my little sister here?"

"She's in her room. Go on in and sit down there at the table, and I'll go get her. You can have the big chair with the arms on it."

I figured the big chair was the one Dad used when he came a-courting, so I felt a little funny sitting in it. When April followed her mother into the kitchen, I stood up and said, "Hi, young lady, I'm Gene. I met you a couple of days ago."

"At the funeral home where my daddy was. You're my brother, like Jesse is."

"That's right, same as Jesse. I call him Jess for short."

Lillian said, "Sit down, Eugene. I fixed you a couple of sandwiches. Is milk okay, or do you want me to fix you some coffee?"

"Milk's fine." I turned to April and said, "What grade are you in?"

"Sixth." She was a pretty little girl with bright blue eyes and sandy hair, and from her looks there was no doubt who her daddy was.

"What's your favorite subject?"

"Arithmetic."

"I never was much good with figures. I didn't have enough fingers and toes."

My awkward attempt at humor was unsuccessful. April said, "I made a hundred on my last test. Are you and Jesse gonna catch whoever killed my daddy?"

"I sure hope so, honey."

By way of changing the subject, Lillian said, "Here's some nice potato salad. Go ahead and get started and I'll be there as soon as I take my apron off."

After lunch, we all had strawberry ice cream and then Lillian and I dragged a couple of ladder-back chairs into the yard and sat in the shade to have our talk. I said, "You've got a real sweet girl there, Miss Lillian."

"Thanks. What was it you wanted to talk to me about?"

"I don't really know. I guess I should ask you if Dad ever talked to you about any sheriff's business or personal business where maybe somebody was mad at him."

"The Blankenships, my trashy in-laws, were really mad at him after he killed Harold out there on the street in Marion, but that was a long time ago. I haven't heard anything out of them in years, and your dad never mentioned them to me."

"Did he ever mention anything to you about a big moonshine operation in Crittenden County?"

"No."

"Did he ever say anything about some men named Green—Cholly and Monkey Green?"

"No. I'd remember a man named Monkey."

"It's a nickname for Montgomery. Did he say anything about some crooks from up in Illinois somewhere?"

"No. Do you think he was killed by somebody from up there?"

"I really don't have any idea. Have you ever been interviewed by any revenuers? Treasury agents?"

"No."

"Have you noticed two men hanging around here? Big hats, driving a black Hudson."

"No, but now you're scaring me, Eugene. Are those men criminals? Is April in any danger?"

"No, they're government agents, so you all aren't in danger. They're from out West, so they wear cowboy hats. If they show up at all, they'll just want to ask whether you know anything about moonshine."

"Well, I don't, and even if I did I wouldn't tell them anything."

"Tell me this, Miss Lillian, was Dad good to you and April?"

"He sure was, especially to April. More like a grandpa than a daddy, really. She's cried her eyes out ever since we came back from Marion the other night."

"Well, he never had a girl to raise, so maybe it was a good thing for him and her both."

Lillian wiped some tears off her cheeks and said, "He sent me money every month, but I've got a decent job and I could've gotten along without it." She looked about a thousand years old, but she couldn't have been but about forty.

"Maybe there'll be something for you all in his will. If there's not, I'll see if me and my brothers can help you out some."

"That'd be nice," she said, but her eyes were focused on a tree branch about six feet over my head.

I got the message that the interview was over, so I looked at my watch and said, "Well, I need to get on down the road."

"Drive carefully, Eugene."

My sweet bastard baby sister ran to the door and waved good-bye to me as I drove away. All of a sudden I felt an overpowering sorrow for her and for myself too, but I got over it by the time I crossed the Tradewater bridge back into Crittenden County.

CHAPTER 22
LITTLE CHOLLY AND JESUS

As soon as I finished my chores the following morning I telephoned the Hopkins County Sheriff's Office for some help locating Little Cholly Green. The sheriff promised to try to find him and call me back.

At about ten o'clock, a deputy called from Dawson Springs to say that Little Cholly and his wife and her daughter were living in a little house on a side road between Dawson Springs and Beulah. He said, "If you come up 70 and turn right at Beuly and head towards Dawson Springs, there's a little road that turns off to the left as soon as you go past a big stand of cedars. It's about two mile out of Beuly. The fellow you're looking for lives in the third house on the left, more like a shack, really."

"Much obliged. Tell your boss thanks."

"Let us know if you want us to pick him up. Sheriff says he don't want no breach of the peace if you should happen to pay a visit to that old boy."

"My intentions are strictly peaceful."

I drove up Highway 70 and, stopping at a general store in Beulah, asked the storekeeper to make me a cheese sandwich. I got a Pepsi-Cola out of the drink box and sat on the front porch and ate my lunch. Then I headed toward Dawson Springs and turned left onto the dirt road that was just past the grove of cedars the Hopkins County deputy told me about. I wondered how Little Cholly would react when he saw me.

I pulled into the yard and honked the horn. Cholly's bony wife squinted out the front door and I said, "I'm Gene Taylor from over in Crittenden County and I was wanting to talk to Cholly."

"I know who you are and I know Cholly don't want to talk to you. You need to get on out of here now, or I'll send for the sheriff."

"The sheriff's the one who told me how to find this place. I don't mean Cholly any harm, so how about just telling me where I can find him."

The woman looked mighty grouchy, but she said, "He's in one of the back fields helping Mr. Poindexter string some bob wire. I guess you can get back in there in your car if you just take and follow around that fence row yonder."

There were two men with Little Cholly, standing next to a team and wagon, and all three eyeballed me suspiciously. I looked at the older of the two strangers and said, "Are you Mr. Poindexter?"

"Who wants to know?"

"I'm Eugene Taylor. I'm a deputy over in Crittenden County. I'd like to talk to Cholly for a minute, if you can spare him. I won't be long."

"If he don't care, I don't care." He looked at Cholly.

Cholly was skeptical. "Eugene, I don't want no trouble with you. I moved up here to get away from my wicked life and I done found Jesus."

"I'm not looking for trouble. Step over here and sit in the car with me for a minute."

"Mr. Pinedexter's paying me to string fence wire, not jaw with you."

Mr. Poindexter cracked his knuckles and looked aggravated. "I done said I don't care if you talk to this boy, just make it snappy. We're burning daylight here."

"Okay, Mr. Pine, I'll be back directly."

Cholly and I walked to the car and got in. I said, "So you got religion?"

"I did, praise Jesus."

"When did you see the light?"

"I first seen the light when you brained me with that rifle butt out there in the snow last winter. When you was beating on me, it was like a demon from hell was a-clawing at my liver. I couldn't holler and I couldn't move, and there wasn't nothing for me to do but just lay there and take it. That's when I knowed I was a lost soul."

"Like Saul on the road to Damascus."

"That's right, just like that! So as soon as I could get up and about again I went to church and taken Jesus as my savior, but I had to wait till warm weather to get baptized. By then I'd moved up here close to my wife's folks. I go to church ever Wednesday night and twice on Sunday."

"As long as all that old stuff's in the past, what happened between you and Bob that day? Bob never would tell me."

"Well, I hate to admit it, but I was in the moonshine business out there in the bottoms by Riley Springs, you know. I was selling a little of it around home, but most of it was going out of county."

"Where was it going, up into Illinois or somewhere like that?"

"I don't know, just away from Crittenden County somewheres. A couple of fast-talkers in a reefer milk truck would come by and pick up a load once in a while. Now I think about it, I believe the truck did have Illinoise license plates."

"So how did you and Bob get crossways of each other?"

"Well, we agreed a couple of days beforehand that I'd meet him over there early that morning and sell him a gallon of whiskey. I didn't want to get out of bed after I seen that ice bark, but I figured nothing would stop that old rascal from coming over there to get his whiskey, cold weather or no cold weather. So I slipped and slid over there in the snow and ice and, shore enough, there he was a-waiting on me. He wanted a drink right away to warm hisself up, so I handed him the jar and he taken a quick drink and then dropped it and busted it. His hands was cold I reckon, but then he didn't want to pay me. I'd walked over there in the snow and my feet was cold and I wanted my money and I took it, plus a little extra for my trouble. I hope the Good Lord'll forgive me for what I done."

"Did my father know about the whiskey still?"

"Why, course he did, Eugene. I thought all of you all knowed about it. That's why I asked you if Ross knowed you was out tracking me in the snow."

"I was tracking you because you beat the hell out of a good old man." It still pissed me off to think about it.

Little Cholly looked down at the floorboard. "You're right, that's what I done and I hope I don't go to the Bad Place for doing it, but that old scamp put up a heck of a fight. I thought I'd have to kill him to get him to quit coming at me. He's old and gray, but he's tough as a boiled anvil! Ever time I knocked him down he'd bounce back up and keep a-coming." Knowing Bob, I wasn't surprised to hear this news.

"So was Dad in on selling that whiskey out of county?"

"He was the big boss, God rest his soul. He's the one who told me when to look for the milk truck."

"Have you got any idea who killed him?"

"Nope, not unless he got hisself in a pickle with them boys who was buying up all the whiskey. They was awful bossy and smart alecky."

"Have you seen any revenue agents snooping around since you moved up here?"

"No and I don't want to see none, neither!"

"Have you seen two men in a black Hudson?"

"No, we don't get many Hudsons up in here. Why?"

"They're revenuers."

"Well, if I see 'em, they for shore ain't gonna see me. I can go places that Hudson can't go."

"Do you think Big Monkey would know anything about the smart-alecky boys in the reefer truck?"

"You could ask him, but I don't think so. He's kissed and made up with his wife and they're trying to do a little farming out there at the home place. Her arm's pert near good as new. I don't think he's making any whiskey or doing much else crooked. He didn't like it none over at Eddyville. Says it ain't near as nice as the county jail. Says the guards over there at the Wall don't have no sense of humor."

"Has he gone to church with you yet?"

"No, but I'm a-working on it. Me and Jesus is."

CHAPTER 23

THE BLANKENSHIP FAMILY

I wanted to talk to Bob Martin about the murder and the moonshine, so the next day I drove to his place for a confab.

"Bob, how long were you in the Army?"

"Twenty-seven years. I got out in nineteen and nineteen and come on back here. I was raised over close to the riffle in Big Piney, but my family's all dead and gone. The Army wouldn't send me overseas for the Great War on account of I had a double rupture, but I taught a whole bunch of doughboys how to shoot. Spent most of the war at Camp Shelby, Mississippi."

"Did you make any rank?"

"Corporal when I got out. Sergeant two or three different times, but ever time I got promoted I'd get busted again. I was bad to drink and fight, but I never got caught stealing nothing."

"I remember you used to tell me you were in Cuba and the Philippines."

"Yeah, I was at Santiago. That's where San Juan Hill's at, you know, and then about six months later they put us on a slow boat to the Philippine Islands. Douglas MacArthur's pappy was an Army big shot over there, but he didn't get along with old William Howard Taft. He was a soldier, you know, and Big Bill was just an old blubber-gutted civilian. You know, sometimes it seems like all that stuff was only yesterday, and other times it's like it never happened at all."

"I know what you mean. Say, Little Cholly Green told me about the little scuffle you and him had out there in the snow by Riley Springs."

"I would've whipped his ass if I was thirty years younger. There was just too much of him and not enough of me."

"How come you never wanted to tell me about that little episode?"

"Well, I was ashamed of myself, craving that whiskey the way I done, and then dropping the jar and busting it, and then trying to chisel Little Cholly out of his money. I didn't want you to scorn me over it."

"Bob, you're just about the best old man in Kentucky, and I wouldn't ever think bad things about you. Now what did you know about Dad's part in this moonshine operation Jess told us about?"

"That's another reason I didn't want to tell you nothing about me and Cholly. Your dad knowed Cholly was making whiskey at that still, and where the whiskey was going, and he was damn shore taking his cut of the money that was being made. I figured it'd hurt you if you found out about it, so I didn't want to tell you. Now I guess it don't matter so much."

"No, it don't matter much at all. Now listen, Bob, I need you to stay far away from anything remotely connected with moonshine. Don't drink it, don't buy it, don't sell it, don't talk about it, don't think about it, and don't go within a hundred miles of where somebody's making it or selling it. If you need a drink, I'll take you to Morganfield or Paducah and buy you some whiskey that's got a tax stamp on it."

"Well, I really do like old pop-skull better than the boughten kind, but I expect I can drink red whiskey if I have to. Hell, I reckon

I've drunk about everything there is at one time or another. How come all the excitement?"

"There've been some revenue snoopers around here that I think would shoot first and ask questions later, and I don't want them to get to woofing after you."

"Neither do I. You know, if we leave right now we can get to Morganfield and back before dark."

"I'll take you over there tomorrow afternoon. How come you think it was one of the Blankenships who killed my father?"

"It's just a feeling I've got. Old Man Blankenship's got a big mouth and he's been talking tough for years. He's nothing but a bag of wind but he could've got one of the younger boys fired up to do something crazy."

"I guess we'll keep them in mind, no matter what Jess says."

"I believe I would if I was you."

Old Man Blankenship and his wife had eight children. The oldest was Harold, nicknamed "Boots" (the one Dad killed). Then came Hershell, Eva Nell, Pearl, Juanita, the twins Weed and Wedge, and Eddie Ray. All but Hershell and his family lived in town in the tough little neighborhood called Crackshin, close by the Illinois Central railroad tracks.

The old man was shiftless. He drove an old horse and wagon around town picking up junk, and in the springtime, he'd hitch the horse to a plow and break ground for people's vegetable gardens. Hershell, the white sheep of the family, drove a dump truck for the West Kentucky Fluorspar Company and stayed as far away as possible from the rest of his family.

Eva Nell and Pearl were married and had numerous children. Juanita—who was not married, but had numerous children nevertheless—lived with Eva Nell and her husband. Eva Nell (also known as "Evil Nell") took in washing and ironing, but neither of the other girls worked at anything other than staying pregnant.

The twins Weed and Wedge (Christian names unknown) were layabouts who lived with their parents. The youngest boy, Eddie Ray, also lived with the old folks, but had a steady job working at the gas station on South Main.

I thought a lot about what Bob said about the Blankenships, so one evening about a week later I ate my supper and went in early for the night shift. I drove into Marion on 120, turned right on Mulberry Street and then right again into Crackshin. I stopped on the cinder street in front of the Blankenship residence and went up and knocked on the door. I could hear a radio playing inside, but nobody responded to the knock. I pounded a little louder and the door was flung open by Old Man Blankenship himself. Angry and stupid, he glared at me and said, "I know you—you're one of them Taylor whelps! What the hell do you want?"

"I . . . we're trying to figure out who killed my father, and I just wanted to talk to you for a minute."

"Your God damned father stole my boy's wife and then took his life, so I got nothing to say to you or no other cops neither. I'm glad he's dead and I don't know nothing about who killed him, except whoever done it ought to get a medal."

"Where were you the night it happened, Mr. Blankenship?" I was having a major problem controlling my temper, and I already suspected I'd made a big mistake ever coming into Crackshin.

"Me and my wife and my boys—except for Hershell—was all at home the night it happened, and my daughters was home too, with their husbands and kids. So we don't know nothing, but I can tell you we all had a jubilee when we heard the news. It's just a damn shame your old mammy didn't get it too."

Enough was enough, so I smiled at him and said, "Don't say another word, you old son of a bitch, or you'll be in hell before breakfast."

There may have been something about my words or my expression that caused Old Man Blankenship to feel the cold fingers of death wrapped around his heart, because his eyes got real big and he slammed the door in my face. I could hear fast footsteps moving back through the house.

So did one of the Blankenships kill my father? The old man was definitely a bag of wind, but would he have the moxie to do murder? Was there any reason to suspect Hershell or Eddie Ray, who seemed to be more-or-less productive members of society? Did the worthless twins, Weed and Wedge, have enough ambition to plan an assassination? Could Evil Nell have found a way to take revenge for the death of her big brother? I decided that the answer to all these questions was *probably not*. The best bet was still gangsters from over in Southern Illinois.

CHAPTER 24

THE WILL

We were sitting in Mr. W. G. Robertson's office in Princeton, waiting to have Dad's will read aloud to us. Mr. Robertson had always taken care of all of Dad's legal matters. He was an imposing presence, tall and distinguished with his greying hair and his rimless glasses. He cleared his throat and began to read, stopping from time to time to explain all the legal mumbo-jumbo.

According to him, the will asserted that Ross Taylor was of sound mind and disposing memory and that he wanted Jess to be his executor. By way of explanation, Mr. Robertson said, "Jess, you've got a legal duty to locate all your dad's assets and pay all his lawful debts. He's forgiven any debt that may be owed to his estate by any of you all or by Miss Lillian Blankenship." Mom looked straight ahead and Mr. Robertson soldiered on.

The next part of the will dealt with the big house and the 600-acre farm, plus livestock and machinery. He looked at Mom and said, "Miss Lera, according to this provision of the will, you're the sole owner of the farm and all the livestock and machinery."

"Very generous of him to leave me my mama and papa's farm."

"Ah . . . yes ma'am," said Mr. Robertson, and he went on reading. We learned that Jesse Coop Taylor inherited the Taylor Hardware

Store and Lumber Yard, and Haskell Francis Taylor got the Taylor Funeral Home. Me, I was to receive the half interest in the flour mill and any personal car and any riding horse that Dad owned at the time of his death. Lillian Blankenship got $1,000.00, and little April got a respectable little trust fund.

"I believe this part of the will is self explanatory," Mr. Robertson said.

Mom looked at him coldly. "I believe it is."

Next, Mr. Robertson informed us that Dad had bequeathed to the County of Crittenden a 1940 Ford patrol car, three Model 37 Ithaca shotguns, and certain two-way radio equipment, sirens, and red lights, all of which he'd bought with his own money.

Finally, according to Mr. Robertson, Dad left half of the rest of his estate to Mom, and one-tenth each to Jess, Hack, Lillian, April, and me.

Mr. Robertson set the will down on his desk and took off his glasses. "This instrument was properly executed in the presence of two witnesses on the second day of February, 1942."

Bequeathing me a horse was Dad's joke from beyond the grave. He did in fact own a saddle horse at the time of his death and it was none other than the old chestnut racking horse, Ruby Laffoon. Ruby was over twenty years old but Dad had boarded him with some people who took good care of him, and he was still a nice-looking piece of horseflesh.

About a week after the will was read, I got Irene to take me into town and drop me off at the stables where Ruby had been kept. I paid the man what Dad owed on his bill, plus a little bonus for all his good work. He helped me with Dad's saddle and bridle, and I mounted up. The stirrups had to be taken up considerably to accommodate my short legs. I rode around the paddock for a couple of minutes to get myself used to being horseback, then out the gate toward home.

Ruby wasn't as snorty as he was when he was young, but he still showed some spirit, so I let him rack a little on the flat stretches of road. I wondered if he was humiliated to have a man on his back who rode humped over like a frog. When I got home, I wiped him down and turned him into the pasture with the maiden-lady mules Kate and Belle. They were enchanted.

Irene started throwing up in the mornings and feeling sluggish. I took her to see the doctor one day and he told us she was pregnant. She had been wanting a baby and so had I, but I was worried I wouldn't be a good father, afraid I'd end up being the kind of a sorry parent Dad was, afraid all the killing I'd done in my life would blight the baby somehow. I kept my concerns to myself, though, because I didn't want to put a damper on Irene's joy.

Not long after the visit to the doctor, I got a letter from a guy I didn't know. He said he was a college student up in Indiana, and he wanted to thank me for saving his life. According to him, he was a replacement BAR man in my company. He said he and the other men were scared of me, but they all looked up to me and thought I didn't know the meaning of fear. He obviously didn't know how many times I screamed like a girl and pissed in my britches because I was so scared.

He went on to say that in December of '44 he was in an outpost in the snow when he got his arm shattered by a big shell fragment. He claimed I ran out to him and got a tourniquet on his arm and popped some morphine into him and called for an aid man and fired on some Panzer grenadiers with his BAR. Clearly a fantasy on his part, because I didn't remember anything about the alleged incident and I didn't remember anything about him.

He ended up by saying he'd met a girl in school that didn't mind having a one-armed boyfriend and they were going to get married in the summer and both of them were going to be school teachers and all that was possible because of me.

Well, when I finished reading the letter I started crying and I couldn't stop. I cried because of what he said about me that either never happened or I couldn't remember it, and I bawled because there was so much rough stuff back then that it was maybe just all in a day's work. And I wept for that brave boy who was going right on with his life like nothing had happened to him, just like old Tuck the three-legged dog. Nobody saw me crying.

At first I didn't know how to respond to his letter. I had a sneaking suspicion I may have been the man who sent him out to that snowy outpost in the first place. I had to do that a lot with new men, so I didn't want to know their names or anything about them. I thought maybe that way I wouldn't feel so bad if they got killed. I'm probably the fellow who got him shot, yet here he was writing me this nice letter.

The thing that happened to that boy over there in the snow was important—to him at least—and I didn't think I ought to ignore it, so when I came home early the next morning after work I sat down at the kitchen table and wrote a reply:

Shady Grove, Ky.
9 Nov. 1947

Mr. Chester Collins (Student)
Indiana State Teachers College
Terre Haute, Ind.

Dear Chester Collins:

Thank you for your letter of 2 Nov. and the kind words it contained.

I remember you as a brave and faithful soldier, and I am proud to have had the opportunity to serve with you.

I wish you every success in the future.

Sincerely,
E. O. Taylor

Some of what I wrote was a big fat lie, but it seemed like the right thing to do. Nevertheless, it got me to stewing again about all the men I've killed and maimed in my life. The one-armed boy's letter knocked the scab off some memories I dreamed about at night and tried not to think about during the day.

The crying jag made me wonder if I was cracking up. I needed to talk to somebody, but I didn't want to go to a head shrinker.

CHAPTER 25

MY STORY

A few days later, Brother Draper and I were sitting on the highest point of Pine Knob Bluff, looking over at the autumn leaves on the other side of the bottoms. "I brought along a little bottle of truth serum," I said.

"That's okay, but I didn't know you were a drinking man."

"I'm not usually, but I thought a little nip might help me get started, you know, loosen my tongue. I bought it in Morganfield the last time I was over there."

"Why don't you have a sip, then?" It must be remembered that this was not your ordinary Kentucky preacher talking. He'd been jaded by his dealings with the Marines during the war.

I broke the seal on the half pint and took a drink. I made a face and tilted the bottle toward the preacher, who shook his head. I said, "Irene's been hounding me to come and see you for quite a while, ever since the day you came and talked to me out there in the hayfield and then drove me up to the house and ate dinner with us. She thinks I ought to talk to somebody about the war."

"That sounds like a good idea. Where all did you serve?"

"Well, I was in a parachute infantry regiment. I jumped into Sicily, and then Italy, and then France, and then Holland. I was in Belgium, winter of '44, and then on into Germany later in '45. Spent time in the hospital here and there. I'd get shot or cut or punctured, but never enough to get sent stateside. I usually got the hell out of the hospital as quick as I could and found my way back to my old unit before the Army could send me to a replacement depot. I wanted to be with the boys in my company—them that were still alive, anyway."

"They say you got a bunch of medals."

I squinted at the label on my bottle of truth serum. "I got an award once for puking the most in a C-47."

"Do you think you're different now from the way you were before you went overseas?"

"Well, before the war, I could get a good night's sleep, and my hands didn't shake, and I wasn't mad at people all the time. And I could go out in the woods on a snowy day without getting the heebie-jeebies."

"Looking back, what was the worst thing about the war?"

"Besides being away from home, the worst thing was all the good boys we left in the graveyards over there."

"Well, Gene, you've got to remember the Good Lord's the one who decided who got to come home and who didn't. Did you feel bad when you took other men's lives?"

"I was scared plumb to death all the time, and the scareder I was, the madder I'd get. I wanted to throw my rifle down and run, but I couldn't stand to be a coward, and that pissed me off too. After I was a sergeant, I got to where I tried to take care of a lot of business myself because I didn't want to be the one to get somebody else killed if I could help it. You may not believe it, but I could smell a German before I could see him—leather and wool and whatever they used for tobacco—but some of those new boys didn't have sense enough to take care of themselves."

"Remember the centurion in the Bible. *I am a man under authority, having soldiers under me, and I say to this man, Go and he goeth; and to another, Come and he cometh; and to my servant, Do this, and he doeth it.* Somebody had to be the Centurion, and all you could do was the best you could do."

"Every time I woke up I figured I was fixing to die that day, so what was left of my mind just spiraled off to a place where I meant to kill everybody that got in my way, and that's what I did. I killed one—just a boy really, only seventeen years old—with my bare hands. Strangled him while he was hacking away at me with a knife. He was trying to get at my neck but I dug my chin into my collarbone and all he got was my face. After he went unconscious I cut his throat with his own steel. I still think about how young he looked there in the snow with all that blood, dead blue eyes bugged out and looking right at me. Some German woman's baby boy who wouldn't ever be going home."

Brother Draper handed me his handkerchief, and we sat quietly for a while. Then he said, "I think it's important to remember you were in a war, and you were killing men who were trying to kill you."

"That's true, but I knew of a fellow who busted a cap on a couple of SS officers he'd captured. Them or some of their pals murdered some GI's and a bunch of Belgian civilians and *then* they wanted to surrender, so this guy I'm telling you about marched those bastards into a thicket and disposed of them. One was crying and hollering, *Nicht schiessen, nicht schiessen,* but the other one just stood there and took his medicine, the arrogant son of a bitch. The one that was hollering got shot first."

Brother Draper looked like he wanted to say something, but once I started talking I couldn't seem to stop.

"And later on, right at the end of the war, this same guy killed a big fat Nazi civilian who'd gotten up to some meanness. Beat his head to jelly with his rifle butt and then got him buried in a hurry and the captain wrote it down as a suicide. He said that old square-head must have got to feeling so ashamed of himself he beat his own brains out."

Brother Draper knew very well I was talking about myself and not some other guy, but he kept up the charade. "I'm sure the Good Lord will forgive that fellow, whoever he was."

"Well, there's more. There was some killing in Berlin after the war was over."

"What on earth for?" It seemed that even Brother Draper at his best wasn't ready for this.

"Some men just needed to be killed, is all I can tell you."

Brother Draper looked at me and shivered. Then he patted my shoulder, and that was all the talking we did about the war. He'd heard enough to know he'd heard enough.

So here's the rest of it.

I had enough points that I could have come home as soon as the Germans cried uncle, but a certain high-ranking officer personally asked me and a few others to stay for a while and take care of a little job for him. I admired that officer, whose name I'll never tell, and if he asked me to do a thing for him I would do it or die trying.

It seems that our former friends the Russians were behaving badly in the U.S. Zone of Occupation in Berlin, and this officer wanted something done about it without provoking some kind of an international incident. According to him, a good Ivan was merely a dangerous drunken bully while a bad one was a looter or a rapist or a murderer, or all of the above. German civilians in our zone weren't safe from them and neither were the GI's. They ran roadblocks and shot at everything that moved, and they knocked old people down for the gold in their teeth, and they violated every woman they could catch.

My little group was officially called an honor guard, but we didn't do much honoring or guarding either. We had our quarters out in the city away from other military personnel, and during the day we slept and read and played cards. At night we crept out to put the chop on any misbehaving Russians we found in our zone. Not to put too fine a point on it, we were a death squad.

We did our job quietly and efficiently. Our preference was to use cold steel on them so there'd be no noise to attract the attention of our own Military Police, but otherwise we just shot them and dumped their bodies into an alley or a canal.

We usually operated in small teams when we were on our mission, but I happened to be all alone one time when I became involved in a dispute with three or four drunk Russians who had decided to have their way with a little old German girl. I didn't know any Russian except *Da* and *Nyet*, and they didn't appear to speak any English, so really there wasn't much of a conversation. One of them died with his britches around his ankles and the rest were last seen headed east.

After I shot that first one down and the others lit out for the Soviet zone, the frightened girl looked at me like she thought I was maybe going to start up where they left off. I just jerked my head to show her which way to go in case she didn't know, and she grabbed what was left of her clothes and took off. I put a couple more rounds in the deadster's head and got the hell out of there in case his comrades came back with some reinforcements. That lustful Russian was the last man I killed in Europe.

Irene was right about one thing. It was easy to talk to the preacher who used to be a Navy chaplain. He was a kind man who understood war and he didn't propose to sit in judgment of me or anybody else. But it didn't make me feel a bit better to spill my guts to him and I still had the bad dreams, so I guess my good wife was wrong about that part. I think the dreams were like a safety valve on a steam engine. Maybe they bled off a little pressure from where my head was boiling around inside.

One reason my brain was in ferment was the secret knowledge that I kind of enjoyed a lot of the killing. I slaughtered a bunch of men and—with some exceptions such as Kraus, the Catholic kid from Bremen—killing them didn't bother me any more than chopping a weed out of the garden.

Young Kraus and I had a primitive life-and-death struggle to find out which of us got to keep standing on his hind legs, and I felt sad when I thought about him. Other men I killed because, in my opinion, they just needed killing. Those were the ones I enjoyed. Suffice it to say that the man who came back from the war bore little resemblance to the Kentucky farmer boy who didn't like to see the hogs killed and hung up in the smokehouse.

CHAPTER 26

THE HOLIDAY BLUES

One Sunday after the Christmas holiday I didn't feel like doing anything constructive and I wasn't sleepy, so I whistled up old Whitey and put him in Dad's Buick and we took a drive. Whitey liked to have the window down, so the ride was a little breezy. Eventually I found myself on the Cave-in-Rock Road. When I got down to the landing I pulled off the road and watched the ferry beat its way from the Illinois side back across the river.

The Ohio was booming from some recent heavy rains and the pilot was having to work hard. It took him quite a while to get back to the Kentucky side, and as he approached the landing he had to judge the swift current exactly right so he could mate up the ramp of the ferry with the ramp of the landing. The ramps came together with a clash and he gunned the diesel engine to hold them together while the mate flipped heavy chains over the cleats to hold the ferry fast so the cars could drive off. A nice piece of work!

The river was out of its banks, filled with driftwood and other debris. As the ferry backed away from the ramp and headed back across to the Illinois side, I saw a partially submerged tree come sweeping downstream not far from where I was parked. Perched high in its branches was a big possum, holding on tight with his tail and all four feet.

Now a possum isn't a handsome beast under the best of circumstances, so you might expect this one to look particularly miserable and bedraggled, but this was not the case. I swear he looked pleased and proud, like some famous person in a ticker tape parade. That got me to thinking, why shouldn't he be happy? Even if he didn't know exactly where he was headed, he was alive and moving downstream, and there was a good chance his tree would sooner or later find its way to solid ground on the river bank or maybe on Hurricane Island, just a little way downstream.

On the way back to town, I thought about how life was going to be without my father. I was surprised at how hollow I felt inside. Some of it was just the holiday blues, I guess, but there was no doubt Dad had left a vacuum when he died.

Another thing worrying me was I still didn't know what I was going to do about the moonshine operation he'd masterminded, or whether Jess was going to try to keep it going. If the boys from Little Egypt liked Crittenden County whiskey and they were making money selling it, they'd be pretty mad if their source dried up. And for all I knew they'd killed Dad in some kind of dispute over how things were being run. That was still our best working theory, anyhow.

Myself, I really didn't care if people made a little whiskey, even if it was against the law. On the other hand, I didn't like a bunch of tough guys coming into the county and turning the whole thing into a racket. And I didn't like them killing my father, either, if they were the ones who did it.

The way I saw it, there were a number of different things I could do with regard to the whiskey problem. The simplest thing, of course, would have been just to keep my mouth shut, mind my own business, and keep on being a deputy. A problem with that theory was that Burl C. Appling and Doughball McKelvey were liable to come back, shoot me full of great big holes, and throw me down into the creek mud.

Or I *could* keep my mouth shut and mind my own business and quit being a deputy and just be a farmer. There was still the danger that Burlap and Doughball would hunt me down and kill me or send me to the Atlanta Pen. After all, why should they believe I wasn't involved with Jess in the Little Egypt conspiracy?

Or I could go to Burlap and Doughball and tell what I knew about my brother and the Illinois gangsters, but there was no way I was going to do that!

Or I could *tell* Jess I was going to rat him out if he didn't get out of business with the gangsters, and let them be pissed off if they wanted to be. Kill two or three of them on a dark country road and maybe the rest would go on back north of the river and buy their whiskey somewhere else. But even if I did that, I was still in danger from the Appling and McKelvey show.

On a related note, I'd figured out why Dad wanted me to be a deputy so bad. He wanted to keep an eye on me so he could decide whether I'd be inclined to become a part of his and Jess's county crime wave. The big moonshine conspiracy must have been one of the "other investments" Jess told me about when I first came home from the Army. I think Dad may have had it in mind for me to become his hatchet man, but he must have also been afraid I might have a misguided honest streak. I guess he went to his grave wondering what I'd do, and now I didn't know, myself.

CHAPTER 27

SUPPER WITH ALTON
AND ROUGHHOUSE

I continued to sniff around for clues in Dad's murder. On a whim, I went to the County Clerk's office and looked up an address. After I found it, I still didn't know exactly how to get there, so I went over to the Farmers Bank and asked Mr. Bill Lowry if he knew. He used to be the county clerk and I knew him from when I was a kid.

He was a tall gawky man who peered at the world through horn-rimmed eyeglasses, and he had a gold front tooth that glistened when he talked. I showed him the name and address, and he said, "Reginald Watkins? Never heard of . . . Wait a minute, is that Roughhouse Watkins?"

"Yes sir."

"Why in God's name would you want to find him if you don't have to? Has he killed somebody?"

"No sir, but he was one of the main players in a little scrape we had down at the Maude Alice Mine last year, and I want to talk to him about whether any of his bunch is still mad at Dad. I remember Dad telling him how he liked the Watkinses and they went way back, and I don't know what he meant by that."

What I was really wondering was whether some of the Watkinses may have been in the moonshine business with Dad, and whether they knew or suspected anything about who killed him. I was running out of ideas.

Mr. Lowry told me how to find the house I was looking for. It was on a dead-end road that turned off the highway between Deacons Landing and the county line.

The Cumberland River runs past Deacons Landing on its way to where it empties into the Ohio. Like many river towns, Deacons Landing contained a number of rough-and-tumble people who resented any intrusion into their business. I was thinking about this as I drove up to Roughhouse's place late one dreary February afternoon.

Before I ever got out of the car I was greeted by a pack of skinny dogs who were making a lot of noise and by a tribe of ugly but bashful kids. Then Roughhouse himself came out on the porch and walked over to the car. I rolled the window down and held my .45 pointed at him down where he couldn't see it. (You've got to be careful if somebody comes up on you when you're sitting in a car.) He recognized me and said, "You're Sheriff Taylor's gunman, ain't you?"

I didn't care for that remark, but I said, "Well sir, I was backing my father up that day out at the mine, if that's what you mean."

"That's as good a way as any to put it, I reckon. I was sorry to hear about your dad. What can I do for you today?"

"We're just trying to go over everything he got up to in the last couple of weeks he was alive, so maybe we can figure out who killed him. We keep going up blind alleys."

Roughhouse said, "I don't mind talking to you a-tall, but I'd like my brother Alton to be there to help me. He's got a better memory than I do and he can talk better. Let me get my car, and then you can follow me back up to Deacons Landing and we'll talk at his house."

Well, that was a kick in the ass. I was a little bit leery of Alton as a result of the Maude Alice episode, and I hoped I might have seen the last of him. Now here I was going to his house!

I wondered if I was maybe setting myself up to get knocked in the head. If the Watkinses were involved in Dad's murder somehow, they might think I was getting a little too close for comfort and try to get me out of the way. So while Roughhouse was trying to get his old car started, I holstered my .45 and took my little Colt revolver and put it in my jacket pocket so I could keep my hand on it later on when we were talking. You can fire a revolver through your pocket if you have to, whereas an automatic will malfunction after the first shot because the slide can't cycle.

Alton's house was a surprise. It was small, but it had a fresh coat of white paint and a neat yard surrounded by a matching white picket fence. There was no pack of cur dogs rushing out to get us, either. A pleasant-faced woman met us at the door, and Roughhouse introduced her as Alton's wife, Mrs. Tranquil Watkins. She invited us into the house and led us back to the kitchen. "Supper'll be ready in a few minutes," she said. "You all are welcome to stay."

I hadn't come all the way down to Deacons Landing to eat supper, but before I could say anything Roughhouse spoke up. "If you've got a-plenty, we'll just have a bite with you."

About that time Alton came through the back door and set a couple of sacks of groceries down on the kitchen table. I shook hands with him, but I kept my left hand on the revolver in my pocket. I said, "Sorry about hogging in on you right at suppertime."

"It ain't a problem. Trannie can just set a couple more plates. Roughhouse'd rather eat up here than at home, anyhow. You'd know why if you ever eat his old woman's cooking."

"That is a fact," Roughhouse said.

Alton turned to his wife. "Tran honey, Mr. Taylor's the man that took me to jail after I busted that pool cue across Thinhead Guinn's back. Treated me fair and square."

It was a good recommendation and Trannie beamed at me as she began putting the food on the table. By this time I decided I wasn't going to get murdered right away, so I used both hands to operate my knife and fork. After supper, Roughhouse and Alton and I went into the tiny living room and they lit their pipes and I had a cigarette. I still didn't allow myself to get too relaxed.

"Mr. Taylor wants to talk to us about his daddy," Roughhouse said.

Alton puffed on his pipe. "I hated to hear about him getting killed like that."

I put my hand on the pistol in my pocket and said, "Let me just get to the point. Were any of you all still mad at Dad after the thing at the mine was over with?" I wanted to watch their reaction to this question.

They had a reaction, all right. Both of them looked at me in total surprise, and Roughhouse said, "We wasn't *ever* mad at your daddy."

"Well, I thought maybe you were."

"And I'm *telling* you, we wasn't. When you all got out there we was in a big fat mess, all because that old fool Uncle Ambrose blowed out them windows with his shotgun. He had done smacked the tar baby and we was all stuck to it, and your daddy figured out a way to get us unstuck without nobody having to go to the penitentiary or the graveyard."

"But we came within an inch of a gun battle with you all."

"Your daddy was *not* going to get shot by a Watkins that day. He couldn't have been safer in the arms of a angel. Ain't that right, Alton."

"That's right. When we seen it was him, Roughhouse sent word around to all of us and told us not to shoot at him, no way, no how.

Then he told me to shoot any Watkins that tried to fire on him. That's why I was sitting up high there, so I could watch everybody on both sides."

"I didn't tell him he couldn't shoot *you*, though," said Roughhouse, and he and Alton laughed loudly like dogs barking.

I smiled weakly and said, "Well, I had some concerns about that."

Roughhouse wiped tears of merriment from his eyes. "I'll tell you a nice compliment I heard on you, if it'll make you feel any better. After we left the mine that day, Alton said you was the coldest-looking son of a bitch he ever seen in his life."

I didn't think I looked cold and scary, so I was surprised when I heard what Alton said about me, especially since I more or less thought the same thing about him. He looked about as kind-hearted as a steel trap.

". . . so we had some concerns too," Alton was saying. "I was scared to death, sitting out there in the open like that with no cover, because I knowed from the way you was staring at me I'd be the first one who got shot. Plus, you had that .30-30 and all I had was that little carbine."

"It was a .250 Savage, and I've seen a lot of people killed by little carbines like that one you had. But why did you all go to all that trouble to make sure my father didn't get shot? When he said you all went way back, what was he talking about?"

Roughhouse was suddenly serious. "Did you not ever hear about the Hanson Mine disaster?"

"Yeah, but I don't know much about it."

"Well, me and Alton do, because our Pap was down in that mine. I was a grown man then, but Alton was just a little feller. After the shafts filled up with water and muck out of that big pit, Ross was out there bossing a passel of them volunteer rescue workers and he slaved like a field hand the whole time, wet as a rat, and him a God damn county judge! A county judge chest deep in that nasty water! I seen him cry like a baby when one of them big pumps got clogged up, and I don't reckon he ever slept."

I never knew Dad was anywhere close to the Hanson mine. "You got some of the miners out, didn't you?"

"Every last one. For four days, nothing we done seemed to do no good, but finally we was able to drag Pap and all them other men out into the sunshine, and so me and Alton and our sisters had him for another sixteen years before he died. I give Ross the credit for that, because he didn't know how to quit trying and he wouldn't let the rest of us quit. Cussed us like dogs, but he knowed best."

"That's quite a story."

"And it's a true story, so now you know why no Watkins was gonna bust a cap on Mr. Ross Taylor."

On the way back to Marion I had a lot to think about. For one thing, I felt stupid because I had totally misjudged Roughhouse and Alton. They were hard men and used to hard ways, but there was nothing sneaky or evil about them that I could see. I was the sneaky one, in fact, because I'd spent much of the evening pointing a pistol at them and they didn't even know it.

Another problem was that every time I got my father cyphered out, something would happen to throw off my calculations. He was a bad husband and I thought he was a lousy father, except maybe to little April up in Evansville. Moreover, he was a demagogue and a whoremonger and a crook who betrayed the public trust with a bunch of whiskey-running gangsters who probably killed him.

On the other hand, some people thought him a hero, and who could say they were wrong? He was just what he was, take it or leave it, like it or lump it.

I sure did want to find out who killed him, and it wasn't long before I did.

CHAPTER 28

VINITA SHELTON

J ess tossed an envelope at me and said, "Who's this sending you sweet-smelling love letters?"

I felt my ears turning red. "I never got a love letter in my life, except from Irene when I was overseas." I tore open the envelope and read the letter.

Marion, Ky.
March 6, 1948

Mr. Eugene Taylor, Deputy
Court House
Marion, Ky.

Dear Sir,

You don't know me, I am the girl that works over at the soda fountain across the street.

I need to talk to you, but I am afraid this person I know will hurt me if I do. It's about something real bad and I will probably be in trouble when I tell. That's O.K. but I don't want to get killed or beat up. Everybody says you are real rough and mean, that is why I wrote to you instead of somebody else.

Very truly yours,
Vinita Shelton

P.S. I need to talk to you when my daddy's at work, so call me this Thursday a.m. It's my day off. Our phone number is 105J.

"What do you reckon this is about?" I said, showing the letter to my brother.

"I don't know, but I *am* glad to know we've got a deputy who's real rough and mean."

"Fuck you, Jess!"

"Oh relax, for Christ's sake. Just call her up tomorrow and see what she has to say. It's probably about some chicken thief or something."

"I don't know this girl from Adam."

"I imagine you'll find out she's that pinup girl Old Man Entwhistle has got working for him over at the soda fountain. Looks like some kind of an Indian or Mexican, but I can tell you she's some fine piece of work. You can't get through the door in the afternoons over there for all the high school boys swarming around her like gnats around Fido's dick. I know I wouldn't kick her out of bed."

"Why don't *you* talk to her, then?"

"No, she wants you, big boy. Don't worry, I won't tell Irene."

The office door slammed behind me and Jess was left alone at his desk with what I'm sure was another smart comment right on the tip of his tongue. He wasn't taking me or the letter seriously. I think he was puffed up by his high office.

I called Vinita on Thursday morning and asked her to meet me at the office, but she didn't want to come to the courthouse. I didn't want to be seen in public with her either, after the way Jess had ragged me. We agreed that she'd come to the side door of the funeral home and we could meet in one of the private rooms on the second floor.

She proved to be a stunner indeed. Hair as black as Herod's heart, snapping brown eyes, olive skin, pearly teeth with a little overbite, and a Mae West figure. She wore bobby socks and saddle shoes, and she had a maroon-colored scarf tied around her neck.

"You're not from around here, are you, Miss Shelton?"

"Call me Vinita. No sir, I'm not. My daddy and I are from Oklahoma. He was in the penitentiary out there at McAlester when I was a little girl, and after he was paroled he got a job as a coal miner. We moved to Illinois after my mama died, and he mined coal up around Herrin and dug spar at Rosiclare."

"Have you ever heard that part of Illinois referred to as Little Egypt?"

"Sure, that's what everybody calls it."

"Did you go to school?"

"I went to high school at Herrin, and then I worked in a café after we moved down to Rosiclare. How about you, did you go to high school?" Vinita had a bold and curious way of looking right into your eyes, like there was nothing in the world quite as interesting as what you might be going to say next.

"What brought you all to Crittenden County?"

"We moved over here so he could go to work mining spar at the LaRue Mines."

"Where do you all live?"

"Out on Kevil Street, close to the depot."

"You said you've been working for Mr. Entwhistle there at the drug store?"

"That's right, at the soda fountain. Mornings or afternoons, or both. We're open from seven to seven."

"How're you and him hitting it off?"

"Oh, we get along fine, but his wife spends a lot of time at the store. I think she's making sure me and him don't run off to the Hawaiian Islands together."

"What's the chance of that happening?"

"Zero percent."

I figured we'd had enough small talk, so I said, "Now Miss Shelton—"

"Call me Vinita."

"Miss Vinita . . . how old are you, anyway?"

"Twenty-one this coming August. I can't wait."

"Anyhow, about this letter you wrote me, what's this all about?"

Her face clouded up and she began to sob. Suddenly, she flung herself at my feet, clutching at my legs. "I'm sorry! I am so sorry!"

I wasn't expecting this! I jumped back and involuntarily looked around to see if anybody had witnessed her dramatic demonstration. I said, "Now you get up from there and sit back down and tell me what's going on. It can't be all that bad."

"Yes it can! I was in the car with your father when he got killed."

"Come again?"

"I was there when he got killed."

"Well, are you the one who shot him?"

"No."

"Do you know who did?"

"Yeah."

"Well who was it?"

"He'll kill me if I tell you," she wailed, "or else he'll claim it was me who done it and I'll be the one to go to the electric chair, so he says."

I didn't want to give this girl a chance to scare herself anymore, so I shifted gears to keep her talking and also to check out her story. I couldn't believe how calm I was. "Did you by any chance drink any of that wine my father had in the car with him?"

"I never saw any wine. He had a pint of whiskey and I had a taste of that because he wanted me to."

"What did you all do with Dad's wallet?"

"I don't think it got taken. If it did, I didn't know about it. He wasn't supposed to shoot Mr. Taylor, anyway, only just take a picture of us, you know, *together* in the car."

"Vinita, right now I need for you to tell me who shot my father. I'll make sure nobody hurts you and I'll see what I can do to help you out of this jam, but you've got to tell me the truth starting right this minute."

"It was Eddie Ray Blankenship."

Bob was right all along! He said he bet it was one of them damn Blankenships, and he was right! I said, "Now see, telling me wasn't so tough, was it? Let's just hear the whole story now—no notes, no stenographer, no nothing—just me and you having a nice little talk."

"Will I have to go to jail? I don't want to go to jail!"

"You might and you might not. I need to hear this story first."

"You'll be awful mad when you hear some of it."

"Quit stalling and tell me the story, and if you come to a tough spot, just plow your way on through it. Let's hear it now. All of it."

She drew herself up and squared her shoulders like a schoolgirl getting ready to recite her lesson. "Well, here goes," she said. "My daddy met Eddie Ray somewhere, probably at some bootlegger's, and brought him home one evening. Eddie Ray's an old guy, like thirty years old, but I started going out with him because I didn't know anybody else in this town back then. Plus he had a nice car. Later on, some other boys, like college boys, wanted to date me, but they was scared of Eddie Ray."

"He's a scary one, all right. Where's he living now?"

"You go out 120 almost to where it crosses the tracks and turn left on . . . I can't remember the name of the street."

"Mulberry Street?"

"Yeah, and then you turn back to the right and him and some more of his family live in a little house with red shingle siding that's supposed to look like bricks."

In Crackshin, where they've always lived. "What's he driving these days?"

"A black '46 Chevy with a coon tail on the radio aerial and a necking knob on the steering wheel."

"What's a necking knob?"

"You know, a knob on the wheel so you can drive with one hand and pay attention to your girlfriend with the other."

"I never heard it called that."

"You don't know much, do you? Why, I bet you've never been out of this county!" (Vinita obviously considered herself a citizen of the world.)

So far, her story was consistent with the facts we already knew about. She knew about the whiskey we found in Dad's car, and she knew his wallet wasn't taken. And Eddie Ray's car might have been the Chevrolet the cook from the Curve Inn Café saw parked just down the road from the murder scene.

"So what did Eddie Ray get you involved in?"

"Well, he got this bright idea for us to make a bunch of money so we could take off and go to California together and I could be a movie star. He said Mr. Taylor fucked his brother's wife, pardon my French, and fathered a bastard on her, and then murdered his brother, and that he ought to have to pay for it. Said Mr. Taylor had plenty of money and he wouldn't miss the little bit we'd squeeze out of him."

"So he used you to get at my father."

"Right. He told me Mr. Taylor was kind of a hound, if you know what I mean, and it wouldn't take much to get him interested in me. He told me to just bide my time till Mr. Taylor came in the drug store. He pointed him out to me one time, so I'd know who he was."

"How'd Eddie Ray tell you to handle it?"

"He didn't tell me nothing, except I should play up to him. I didn't need any advice on how to do that."

"Go ahead."

"Anyways, he came in a couple of days later and sat in one of those twisted wrought-iron chairs at one of the little tables, and I came around to wait on him. I leaned way over the table and let him look at something I thought he'd like to see, and when I brought his malted milk to him I sat down at the table with him for a minute and crossed my legs to let him see a little something else. Just a little leg, you understand, not the Promised Land or nothing. Sort of like this here."

I shuddered and looked away and said, "Did he make any proposition to you?"

"No. He was a perfect gentleman except for the looking part, and it would've been hard for a man not to look at what I was showing him. You had a good look just now, didn't you?"

"What happened next?"

"Next time he came in, he sat at the counter. It was after lunch and before school let out for the day, so I wasn't busy. I did some more leaning over with my top button unbuttoned, and he did some more looking, and we got to talking. He was real sweet, and I could see he *was* a hound, no offense, just like Eddie Ray said he was. When he told me he was the county sheriff, I acted surprised and asked him was he carrying a gun and was it loaded, and blah, blah, blah. He was wearing a suit and tie, and I asked could I see his gun sometime, and he said anytime, ha ha."

"He was smelling the bee pollen."

"If that means he was getting interested, then yes he was."

"So did he ask you to go out with him?"

"Not for a while, but he started wearing his uniform and badge instead of a suit, and I figured he wanted to show out by looking good in his uniform. He did too. If things had been different, I would've probably flirted with him anyway, even if he was older than my daddy."

It dawned on me suddenly that Vinita Shelton working at the soda fountain was the reason Dad was drinking a malted milk and wearing his uniform instead of a suit that day we were called out for the riot at the Maude Alice Mine. "He wanted you to look at his gun, did he?"

"I think he did. What is it about men and their old guns, anyway?"

"I don't know, you'd have to ask a psychiatrist or something. So tell me, how did you and him get together?"

"We went along like that for a few days, and I could tell he was *really* interested in me. A girl can just tell, you know. We'd kid around and tell some dirty jokes, and I'd touch his arm and talk real confidential, even when I didn't have much of anything to say. He finally asked me would I like to shoot his gun sometime, and I said I was about ready to but I couldn't go during the daytime and was it okay to shoot a gun at night, like after work. He said he thought that'd be a great time to do it. Perfect, in fact."

"Were you all still talking about pistol shooting, or had you graduated to another matter altogether?"

"I think he thought we'd graduated to the other matter."

"So what was the plan for twisting money out of him? What did Eddie Ray tell you was supposed to happen?"

"I was supposed to get him to drive me out to that place by the covered bridge, and Eddie Ray'd be hiding in some sumac bushes with a little Kodak flash camera and when we got our clothes off he'd sneak up and take a picture of us, you know, doing it."

"What a nice idea."

"I thought so at the time, too. I told Eddie Ray he needed to get up there as quick as he could, because I thought Mr. Taylor might be pretty impatient to get down to business. After the flash went off, Eddie Ray was supposed to run like crazy in case Mr. Taylor started shooting. My job was to cry and raise Cain and make him take me home. Later on, Eddie Ray'd make him give us money and then we'd leave for California and never come back."

"Were you planning to stay with Eddie Ray once you all got out to California?"

"That was a bridge I would've crossed once I got there."

"If you were to have a way to get to California now, would you ever be interested in coming back here?"

"Heck no! I don't have nothing here to bring me back."

"What about your daddy?"

"It wouldn't bother me a bit to go off and leave him. I have to lock my bedroom door when he's been drinking. Always have, whenever the door had a lock on it. He really ain't worth the powder it'd take to blow him to the moon!"

I felt a stab of pain at the image of Vinita as a little girl with a drunken father and no lock on the bedroom door, but I couldn't think about that now. "How about Eddie Ray? Would you want to come back and see him?"

"Another no-account son of a bitch! Look, Eddie Ray got me in this jam. I was greedy for money, I admit that, but he lied to me about what he was up to, and he used me, and now your father's dead and he's holding *that* over my head. I'd love to see him in hell."

"He'll get there, the only question is when. Now go on and tell me what happened that night." I hated to have to hear the story, but there was nothing else for me to do but shut up and listen.

"Well, when we closed up I walked home and changed clothes and called Eddie Ray and told him I was meeting Mr. Taylor at nine and he better be in those sumac bushes because I didn't think it'd take long once we got out there. About a quarter till nine, I walked back uptown and met Mr. Taylor out behind the little hotel there on that street that runs down by the post office. His car was parked out back, by the stairs."

"What was the weather like?"

"It was real warm for the middle of September, and that was a good thing because I wanted to wear something that'd get his attention right away."

"So what *did* you wear?"

"A little cotton dress and sandals, and I tied a sweater around my neck, but I didn't wear anything at all under the dress."

"What happened when you got up there?"

"We started out pretending we was really going out to shoot his old pistol, but that didn't last long. He had it with him, stuck in his britches, but this wasn't about pistols any more. He wanted me to take a drink of whiskey and I did and he had one too. Then he wanted me to come up the back stairs to his hotel room for another little drink, but I wouldn't do it and—"

I *really* didn't want to hear the rest of her story.

"—then he started hugging and kissing on me, and he reached around and put his hands on me and pulled me up against him, and he could feel I didn't have anything on underneath. I could tell he was ready too. He wanted to get me in the car and do me right there, but I said no, I wanted to go out in the country somewhere nice and wasn't there an old covered bridge somewhere around here. He said there was, and we got in his big old car and went flying out there."

"Did you all drink any more whiskey?"

"He wanted me to have another drink, I guess so I'd be all primed and ready when we got where we were going. So I took a drink and slid over next to him and let him rub the inside of my bare leg and whatever else he wanted to rub, you know, and I took his pistol out of his waistband and put it on the floorboards over on my side. I thought that might give Eddie Ray a little more time to get gone after the flash bulb went off."

We found his pistol on the floorboard, right where Vinita said she put it. "What brand of whiskey was it?"

"I don't remember."

"So what happened when you all got out there?"

"Okay, when we pulled in there and parked he said he had to pee and he got out and took his jacket and hat off and put them in the back seat and then went down next to the creek somewhere. He came back to the car in a hurry—you could tell he had big plans—and by the time he got there I'd slipped off my dress and I was kind of laying back on the seat. He got in but didn't close the door, and before I knew what was going on I heard this pop and saw a flash and he groaned once and went limp and fell out of the car. I thought at first it was Eddie Ray's camera, but it wasn't."

"What'd you do then?"

"It took me a couple of seconds to figure out what just happened, and then I went crazy. Eddie Ray says for me to get my clothes on and let's get the hell out of there and when I moved too slow he slapped my face and pulled me along to where he'd parked his car. I was carrying my sandals, so I was barefooted in the gravel. I said, *What've you done, what've you done?* and he says for me to shut up or I'll get some of the same tonic."

"Where'd you all go after you got back in his car?"

"He was all excited and laughing and acting like a crazy man and waving his little pistol around, and he drove on out the road a little ways and pulled off to the side and made me give him some right there, the son of a bitch."

That's what the Curve Inn cook and her husband saw on their way home that night. It wasn't a couple of murderous Illinois gangsters after all. It was Eddie Ray and his accomplice girlfriend fornicating in his Chevy, and my father laying dead in a puddle of his own gore just down the road. "How's it been with you and Eddie Ray since then?"

"It's like I'm his slave girl, with him holding all this stuff over my head like I'm to blame for everything, and all I wanted was a little money so I could get out of this hick town and go to California. Now I've got nothing. Really, I've got less than nothing."

"What do you think ought to happen to you now?"

"I don't know. Something, I guess, but I don't know what. I know I didn't do murder and Eddie Ray did. I guess I was really wondering if maybe you could sort of look out for me for a while, you know, till Eddie Ray gets sent to prison or the electric chair, or whatever. He and his family'd be scared of you. I'd be real grateful and I'd be good to you. Maybe I could get a little place to live and you could come see me whenever you wanted. I just need somebody to protect me."

I drummed my fingers on the arm of my chair. "That's a nice offer, but I reckon not. First of all, you were in the middle of a crooked-assed scheme that got my father killed. Second, I love my wife and I don't want anything to do with you. Third, I don't know if I want my father's name dragged through the mud like it would be if all this came out, and I damn sure don't want my mom to have to read all about it in every newspaper in Kentucky. And, for what it's worth, I don't think you *need* protection. I think the world needs protection from you."

"Well, what am I supposed to do then?" She seemed a little insulted and indignant that I'd turned down her offer. I'm sure it had never happened to her before.

"Just relax. I've got a few more questions for you."

She was still huffy about being rejected. "What about? I already told you everything I know."

"Do you remember a couple of cowboy types that were in town a while back? A tall older guy and a fat younger guy?

"Are you talking about Mr. Burlap and Doughball?"

"Well God Damn! How in the world do you know those jokers?"

"Oh, back in Oklahoma when I was real little, my daddy and a fellow named Blackie Wheelwright boosted a gas station and Mr. Burlap got after them. Blackie had an old thumb-buster pistol and for some reason he decided to shoot it out. My daddy said Mr. Burlap just tore Blackie all to pieces with a .351 Winchester."

179

"Well, I can believe that," I said.

"Daddy's always been sort of a coward, even when he's drunk. Said when he saw Blackie hit the ground dead, he was so scared he just covered his eyes up with his hands and waited to die, but Mr. Burlap didn't do nothing but walk up and put the cuffs on him and take him to jail. He got sent to Mac penitentiary, of course, and me and my mama moved to McAlester where she could visit him.

"Mama and Mr. Burlap got to be friends while Daddy was locked up. I think he was sweet on her, and he was a hundred times better man than my daddy'll ever be, but she never would divorce Daddy.

"Mama died after Daddy got paroled, and Mr. Burlap helped him get a job mining coal there at McAlester. And after that, Daddy was Mr. Burlap's snitch. Even after we moved to Little Egypt and over here to Kentucky, Daddy was a so-called *confidential informant*. Between you and me, I think a stool pigeon's lower than a snake's belly."

"What kind of information was Mr. Burlap interested in around these parts?"

"Well, there was supposed to be a big moonshine caper, but I don't know nothing about it and that's all I'm going to say. I've got enough troubles without getting myself a snitch jacket."

"Didn't Burlap come to see you at the soda fountain? Were you an informant, too?"

"No, I was not! I'm no stool pigeon! I never snitched on anybody in my life!"

"But he made a special trip up there to see you, didn't he?"

"That's right, but me and him just talked about my mama, how pretty she was, and how much he thought of her. Said I reminded him of her. Had tears in his eyes, poor old man. I felt sorry for him."

I thought for a minute. "Stay here and take it easy for a little while." I left and walked across the street to see Jess. Closing the office door behind me, I said, "I know you and Dad had a lot of loose money in campaign funds or slush funds or whatever you call them. I want you to go get me twenty-five hundred dollars in cash and put it in my hand in the next fifteen minutes."

"What for?"

"Don't cross me on this, Jess. I need it and I mean to have it right now. If you've got to have a reason, you can say I'm working on closing a circle."

Jess looked puzzled, but he walked across the street to the bank and came back with the money in a little grocery sack. He handed it to me without saying a word. Like he said, he knew how to keep his mouth shut.

When I got back to the funeral home, I went upstairs and found Vinita on the sofa chewing on a hangnail. I sat down next to her and said, "Okay, you've got two choices. I think you'll pick the first one, which is this. There's twenty-five hundred dollars in this sack. I'm going to give it to you and you go right this minute—not tomorrow, not next week—and buy a ticket and ride the bus to Paducah. When you get there, buy yourself a suitcase and some clothes and catch another bus to St. Louis or Chicago or Memphis—I don't care which—and then get on a train bound for Los Angeles and never look back. As far as you're concerned, there never were any such people as Eddie Ray Blankenship and Ross Taylor."

"I like that choice, but what's the other one?"

"The other choice is, I come around some dark night and take you out in the country and cut your guts out and fill your belly with rocks and sink you in Tradewater River."

Her eyes were shining. "I thought it might be something like that." She touched my arm and lingered there for a second, soft as velvet, then gently lifted the money sack from my hand like she was picking a pocket. I believe she wanted me to think about what I was missing when I spurned her proposition. As she put the sack in her purse she said, "Too bad I didn't meet you a long time ago."

"My bad luck if you did."

I meant for Vinita to be scared of me, but it seemed like the threat of having her guts cut out only got her excited. I sat and watched her as she got up and walked away, and I could see how Dad could have gotten caught in her web. She sure knew how to use the tools the Good Lord gave her. As she went through the door, she turned back around and smiled like an angel. "Thanks, sweetie," she said, and then she was gone. Jess was right; she was some piece of work.

I stayed away from the courthouse for a few days, just farming and working the night shift. Then one day when I'd come into town to testify in court, Jess had some news. "Hey, one of the city cops told me your little soda-fountain sweetheart's father came up to City Hall a while back, half drunk and saying she'd run off. Said she sent him a postcard from someplace up north saying she was never coming back and nuts to him."

"So what?"

"So do you know anything about where she went?"

"I expect she flew off on her broomstick. Now shut up about it."

He looked at me and started to say something, but then thought better of it. He shrugged and said, "If that's the way you want it."

I said, "That's the way I want it."

I didn't tell Jess about the piece of registered mail I'd picked up earlier that very day at the post office. Expensive envelope, no return address, my name neatly typed, a card inside with nothing on it but a kiss in bright red lipstick. It was postmarked *Hollywood, California*. I burned it and flushed the ashes down the toilet in the courthouse.

CHAPTER 29

THE .38 OWL HEAD

About a week later, I drove around the road to Bob Martin's cabin. He was fooling around outside when I pulled up, so I waved to him and said, "I've got a box of .45's in the back. How about we see if we can hit anything with this old slabsided pistol of mine?"

He'd always been a little scornful of handguns, being the great rifleman he was, but he was glad for the company and he quickly agreed to a little target shooting. He was actually quite accurate with my .45, firing the pistol with his right hand and keeping his left hand stuck in his britches pocket. After he and I had shot up the box of ammunition, we sat on a log and smoked and talked.

"Bob, did you plant that little redbud tree there by the corner of your cabin?"

"No, it just sprouted up on its own."

"Mom says redbuds are Judas trees. Says after old Judas betrayed Jesus he got to feeling guilty and hung himself on a redbud tree."

"I never seen a redbud big enough to make a very good hanging tree, have you?"

"No."

183

"Do you reckon Judas was a midget?"

"Maybe. Why don't you ask Mom sometime?"

"Ask her your own damn self," he said. "I doubt she'd appreciate a fellow poking fun at her religion."

It was about time for me to make my move, so I said, "By the way, didn't you used to have an old top-break revolver around here somewhere?"

"Yeah, I've still got it. I won it in a card game down in Juarez, Mexico, one time when I was on a furlough from Fort Bliss. By God, them was high old times down there, even after they throwed Díaz out. *Más cerveza pronto*! we'd holler. *Fría, por favor*!"

I had no idea who Díaz was and I didn't care to know, so I tried to keep Bob focused on the subject. "I forget, what kind of a pistol is it?"

"It's a .38 Owl Head."

"Do you have any bullets for it?"

"I do, but they're black powder cartridges, and I've had them about as long as I've had the pistol. I don't even know if they'd go bang."

"Are you interested in giving them a try?"

He was indeed interested and he walked back to the cabin to find the old revolver and the ammunition. When he got back, he broke it down, loaded it, and blazed away at some cans amid a cloud of black-powder smoke. I shot it too, and thought it had a hard trigger, but there were no failures to fire. Ejecting the spent casings from the cylinder, I said, "I might have a use for this item sometime, especially if an old man like you had a bad memory of ever owning it."

Without another word, he dumped the remaining live cartridges out of the box and into my shirt pocket. He struck a match with his thumb, burned the box, and scattered the ashes. He picked up all the cartridge casings off the ground, counting them to make sure he had them all, and he walked over and dropped them down a long-vacant groundhog hole at the far corner of his woodlot. Then he moseyed back over to me and said, "Son, I'm old and I don't remember nothing."

I meant to use the old Owl Head pistol to kill Eddie Ray Blankenship. The world just wasn't big enough to hold him and me both.

CHAPTER 30

AT THE FLOUR MILL

I walked up the stairs to the second floor of the Marion Flour Mill. Tapping on the open door of the business office, I said, "Mr. Coleman, have you got a minute?"

"Sure, Gene, come in and sit down. I ain't seen you since your dad's funeral. How's your mother?"

"She's fine, thanks for asking."

"I've been expecting you long before now. I got a letter from that big lawyer over at Princeton saying Ross had left you his share of the mill. I've been real careful to make sure his interest was protected till you could take it over."

"I know you have and that's why I waited so long before I even came in to see you. I'm not worried about the books, but I'd like to ease into looking the operation over so I can make some halfway intelligent decisions. Sooner or later I'll have to decide if I want to sell my interest or keep it."

"Well, Gene, I'll be honest with you. I was sort of hoping you'd sell out to me."

"I sure wouldn't rule that out, but I don't know enough now to decide either way. So what I'd like to do is start coming by here some during the day to learn the operation, and maybe I could come in at night once in a while—you know, when there's not much happening on my night shift—to look at the books and see if I can't get a grip on the business end. Do you think I could have a key to the front door and the office?"

"You can have a key to anything on the place, I reckon. I'll just start leaving the account books on my desk of an evening when I leave, plus anything else I can think of you might need to read over."

"That'd be great. Would it be okay if I take some notes and maybe write out some questions about stuff I don't understand?"

"Anything you want, son."

"Here's the first question: what do you do when you've got your office window open and a train comes by?"

He blinked furiously and looked at me with one eye and out the window with the other. "I try to shut the window when I hear the train blow for the crossings, but sometimes it gets pretty smoky. Coal smoke and flour dust are a heck of a combination."

I looked out the window. "Boy, the railroad track's right outside the back door. Is that a dock out there to load stuff onto freight cars?"

"Yeah, but we don't use it much. The switch for the spur track is probably rusted shut. Everything from here's pretty much shipped by truck nowadays."

"Uh-huh." I wasn't paying strict attention to Mr. Coleman. What I was doing was looking at a certain house down on the other side of the railroad embankment. It had red asphalt siding that was supposed to look like bricks. There was a black Chevrolet parked in the cinder driveway and it had a coon tail on the radio aerial. It was Eddie Ray's car.

Mr. Coleman had something else he wanted to say. "Uh . . . Gene, you *do* know flour dust will explode just like coal dust, don't you?"

"Wow, what would it take to make it blow up?"

"Well, any kind of grain dust will burn, including flour, and if it catches fire in a closed-up space, there'll be an explosion just like a great big firecracker."

"Would it blow up the whole mill or just some of the equipment?"

"The whole mill could blow if you had a big concentration of dust inside the building and somebody lit a cigarette. You don't want to be striking any sparks in here."

No, sir, I won't. Does the door key fit the back door too? I might want to go out back and have a smoke, and I don't want to blow up my inheritance."

"Well, you wouldn't have a high concentration of flour dust in here at night, but it's still better not to smoke inside the mill."

True to my word, I began showing an interest in the operation of the mill. I came several times a week to talk to the men and watch them work, and it seemed like they were pleasantly surprised at what a nice young gentleman I appeared to be. Many of them had heard tales of my supposed volatile behavior since I came home from the war, so they'd been a bit cautious when I first started coming around.

I also came in at night and sat in Mr. Coleman's big leather chair, making scrawling calculations on a tablet based on information I got from the mill's well-kept ledgers and journals. I began leaving handwritten questions that Mr. Coleman was obliged to answer, even if they didn't seem very intelligent. For example:

Dear Mr. Coleman--Would it be a good idea to get some barn cats in here to deal with mice and rats? What about a couple of blacksnakes? (They are hell on mice in a corncrib).

Gene--The smell of cat piss would drive away our customers, and the snakes would drive away our workers, including me.

Mr. C: I agree about the cat piss, but I still think the snakes are a good idea. Blacksnakes are not poison. What is the best way for me to be able to have a smoke on the back loading dock without blowing up the mill? Would a water bucket be a good idea? Thanks.

Gene, I'll have one of the mill hands put a bucket of sand out there for you, but please be careful. I appreciate it.

Mr. C: Thanks for the bucket. I'll be careful. I notice we make more money in some months than we do in others. What can we do to fix this?

Gene, the farmers will have to grow more grain crops in the winter if we're going to make more money in the winter. This is not likely to happen due to the weather.

Privately, Mr. Blinky Coleman probably thought I was an idiot, but he must have also realized that my total absence of business sense might make for a good deal in his hoped-for buyout of my interest in the mill. For my part, I wanted him to have a clear memory of my being around the mill operation in the daytime and by myself in the office at night. So the questions continued for Mr. Coleman, and to each stupid question he returned a reasonable, if slightly impatient, answer. And he tolerated the cigarette butts in the sand bucket on the back loading dock when nobody else was allowed to smoke anywhere on the premises.

From time to time when I was at the mill office during the night shift, I'd turn out the light and stand by the window overlooking the railroad embankment. At other times I'd sit in the dark out back, kicking my heels against the side of the abandoned loading dock and smoking Lucky Strikes. I was always careful to use the sand bucket.

What I was doing was paying attention to the nighttime comings and goings down in Crackshin and figuring out how I was going to kill Eddie Ray and get away with it.

CHAPTER 31

WHAT ABOUT THAT UNTAXED WHISKEY?

With a baby on the way and bloody murder in my heart, I had to get some resolution to the moonshine problem, so I called Jess one Sunday and asked if I could come out to his house for a talk. When I got there, Mary Ruth fixed me a glass of tea and Jess and I went out to their screened-in porch that overlooked the highway. We made small talk for a while and then I got to the point.

"I want to know what you plan to do about Dad's white whiskey operation."

"That depends."

"What does that mean?"

"Do you want in?"

"No. Do you want out?"

Jess thought about it and said, "I don't know if I could get out even if I wanted to. Them boys north of the river are making a lot of money selling Crittenden County whiskey, and they won't want to give it up."

"Jess, the least of your worries may be your pals up in Little Egypt. Do you remember those yahoos in cowboy hats who hung around town for a few days last year?"

"Nothing but deadbeat poolroom loafers!"

"Not true, my brother. The fact is, they're rogue revenuers who intend to catch or murder everybody involved in your moonshine business. Nothing would please them more than to slit your throat and lick the knife."

"Ah, all them Treasury clowns have got their heads up their asses. Dad fooled 'em for years."

"Well, Dad's dead and you're not smart enough to fool these two. They're scary sons of bitches. Let me tell you about the run-in I had with 'em out on the Tribune Creek bridge."

So I told him.

"I hear you," Jess said, "but the men in Illinois are the ones I'm worried about."

I drained my glass of tea and lit a cigarette. "The men in Illinois can get their whiskey somewhere else."

"I'm afraid Mary Ruth'd end up a widow woman if I done that."

"What if they were to quit wanting Kentucky shine?"

"I don't think that's likely. The big boss over there in Illinois does love to sell our whiskey."

I leaned forward and clenched my fists. "I'll help you if it looks like they want to start something. Sooner or later they'll get tired of carrying their people out of here in pine boxes."

"Gene, it ain't that simple. Plus, I'm making a lot of money ram-rodding the operation."

That's when Jess busted his ax with me once and for all, and all of a sudden I knew what I had to do. "Tell you what, I'm just gonna get out of the law business. I'll sell my half of the flour mill to Mr. Coleman and then I'll just be a farmer and raise my kid out there in the country."

"You could keep your deputy job and just stay away from any-thing to do with the whiskey."

"No, I couldn't. I'll just stay out in the country and ride round and round on the tractor and see you every Christmas, assuming you're not in the federal pen or Mapleview Cemetery. The baby's due around the middle of June, so I'll just work through the end of the month."

"Why don't you quit now, if that's the way you feel?"

"I've got a couple of things I'm trying to wind up, cases I'm working on, and I need a little time to take care of them." (The fact was, I needed to be a deputy for a while longer, till after I landed Eddie Ray in hell.)

CHAPTER 32

YOLK PARKER

I had to be in court a couple of days later and I stopped by to see Jess. "I need you to go across the river and pick up a prisoner," he said. "He's in jail over there, and he's waived extradition."

"Anybody I know?"

"It's Yolk Parker."

Yolk was a local farmer who had made tracks out of the county about six weeks earlier, right about the time they found his wife unconscious in a barn stall out at the Parker farm. Also in the stall was a vicious little Jersey bull called Popeye, and he had blood on his horns. The woman had horn punctures in her groin and back and legs, plus a bunch of broken bones. When they found her, she was caked with blood and manure where Popeye had gored and tossed and wallowed her. The stall door was barred from the outside with a two-by-four.

"They've indicted him for attempted murder," Jess said, "but it may be tough to get a conviction."

"How come?"

"Well, the old lady's memory of what happened is a little shaky, and it's theoretically possible the two-by-four fell and blocked the door shut on its own. It was on a pivot so the stall could be bull-tight

194

if Popeye was being kept in there. If Yolk don't confess to locking her in there on purpose, I doubt the case ever goes to trial."

"How'd they catch him?"

"Oh, he was working at Joppa, down the river there from Metropolis. Managed to get in a little tussle at a kick-and-stab beer joint, and some Massac County deputies arrested his ass. Everybody agrees he ain't a very smart criminal. Told them he thought he might be wanted for something up here. Didn't even ask if his wife was alive or dead, the old fucker."

"So how do you want me to handle it?"

"Find somebody to drive the patrol car while you keep an eye on Yolk. You can pay whoever goes with you five dollars for his trouble. Keep Yolk cuffed and shackled and see if you can't get him to come to Jesus and admit he locked the old woman in there so that bull could kill her."

"What if he won't come to Jesus?"

"Then I guess a guilty man's fixing to go free, ain't he?"

"How bad do you want a confession?"

"Look, I want it pretty bad but I don't want to know nothing about how you get it. Just do it if you can, and make sure he don't *escape*." Jess was sending me a little unspoken message. "Of course, stay within the bounds of the law and human decency."

"Of course. Law and human decency. But what if he ain't guilty?"

"The wicked flee when no man pursueth, Gene. If he wasn't guilty why'd he run?"

As I drove home, I thought about the wicked fleeing when nobody was after them. I knew Yolk Parker and I knew he was wicked, but I didn't know if he was guilty of this particular crime. He was a big, heavy man who'd be in his mid-60's by now. His face was round and smooth and shiny, and when he was walking away from you his bald head looked like an oversized egg. I decided if Jess wanted me to transport him and maybe torture him into a confession, or shoot him while he was trying to escape, I wanted somebody with me who'd be likely to keep his mouth shut about anything that might or might not happen. So when I got home I rang up Central and asked the operator to connect me with a certain number down in Deacons Landing.

"Can I speak to Alton Watkins, please?"

"This is him."

"Eugene Taylor calling, Alton. Am I catching you at a bad time?"

"No sir. Been out pulling weeds and cutting grass all afternoon. Trannie cracks the whip and I jump." He seemed proud of his wife's ferocity.

"I know what you mean. Listen, are you working at the mine tomorrow, or could you help me out with a little matter?"

"I'll help you out if I can. I don't go back to the mine till Tuesday."

"Great. What I need is for somebody to ride over to Metropolis with me to pick up a prisoner. It's Yolk Parker. Did you hear about him?"

"No."

"He's got a farm out on Cottonpatch Hill, off the Fords Ferry Road. His wife got gored by a bull and they think he put the bull up to it some way or other and then lit a shuck for parts unknown. They arrested him at a tavern over there in Illinois."

"Well, yeah, I'll ride over there with you."

"Jess says to pay you five dollars for your time, and you can be a deputy for a day."

"Trannie'll be proud I'm a deputy."

Early the next morning Alton and I set off down Highway 60 toward Paducah. Since he was getting paid, I put him to work driving while I sat over on the passenger side and enjoyed the scenery. By way of being a pleasant companion, I asked him if he'd been in the service during the war, and he told me he'd been in the 149th Infantry, a National Guard outfit that saw action with the 38th Division out in the Pacific. When I heard that, I asked him if he'd known Victor Clawson. It turned out he had, so I told him about the time Jess and Hack and I walked up on the big dynamite-hammering contest between Victor and his brother Raymond.

"That sounds like Victor," Alton said. "He was always a bead or two off plumb. He's the one who took a picture of me out in New Guinea that about got me disowned by my family, or so I thought."

"What kind of a picture was it?"

"Well, some of us was fooling around way out in the boondocks somewheres and we run up on a bunch of savages, real-live headhunters. There was one old woman with them looked like she was about two hundred year old, flabby tits hanging down and hardly a stitch of clothes to her name. No teeth, tattoos all over her, you know. She was a scary-looking old gal, but awful cheerful."

"I like a cheerful woman," I said, thinking about Irene, who had all her teeth and not a thing flabby about her.

"So old Victor rooted around in his musette bag and found this little camera he wasn't supposed to have. He got me to pose for a picture with my arm around this old woman, and her just a-grinning, never mind she didn't have no teeth. It was quite a while before he finally got the film developed, but he give me that picture. Not long after that's when he got killed by that Jap suicide plane."

"So how'd you get in trouble with your family?"

"I only *thought* I was in trouble. You see, Pap had died and Mama was taking it pretty hard. I kept getting letters from Roughhouse and my sisters telling me how sad she was and how it seemed like she didn't have all her wits about her. So what I done, I thought up something I thought would make her laugh. I sent her that picture and a letter with it saying I was engaged to marry that old headhunter squaw, and I asked her could she see about getting a wigwam or something built for us out there in the back yard of our home place. Told her my fiancée wasn't used to living in a house."

"That's funny."

"I thought it was too, till I got this nasty letter from Roughhouse saying Mama believed every word of it. Said she stuck a piece of tape on the picture to cover up the old woman's bosom, and was showing it to everybody at church and asking around to see if anybody around home there knowed how to build a wigwam. I didn't find out till the war was over that Mama and Roughhouse had whipped me at my own game! They really had me believing I was gonna get disowned or else have to live in a wigwam in the back yard the rest of my life."

I was a little surprised. "You don't think about Roughhouse having that kind of a sense of humor, do you?"

"Oh, he's a dry one, Roughhouse is. If some Jap had shot me during the war, I never would've knowed Mama and him was having a big laugh about me and the headhunter dame."

"If you don't mind me saying so, speaking of family, it seems like your Deacons Landing wife's an awful nice girl."

"Yeah, thanks. Trannie, she's a love bunny till you get her riled, then it's time to flee for your life. She runs a tight ship. If it don't move, paint it. Chop chop, hubba hubba. We've only been married a couple of years."

To get to where we were going, we had to cross the Cumberland River at Smithland, then the Tennessee River on our way into Paducah, and then the Ohio River between Paducah and Brookport, Illinois. I'm scared to death of bridges, because of the height and the fact there's water down below, so I was glad Alton was driving. You'd think the fact I was once a paratrooper would signify, but it didn't because I was scared of jumping out of airplanes too.

The Irvin Cobb Bridge over the Ohio there at Paducah is about a mile long and just wide enough for two cars to meet each other without slapping their outside mirrors together, and to make matters worse there's a sharp curve to the left as you get close to the end of the bridge on the Illinois side. When we started across, I pretended I was looking out the window so Alton couldn't see I had my eyes shut. It seemed like we were on that bridge forever.

"Uh, how do we get to the jailhouse, Mr. Taylor?"

"What? Oh, just stay on Highway 45 here and follow it on into Metropolis."

When we picked Yolk up we cuffed his hands in front of him and shackled him and put him in the back seat of the patrol car. I ran his shackle chains through his handcuff chains so he could sit there like a gentleman, but he couldn't get to flailing around enough to cause us a problem.

Once we were back on the Kentucky side, I got right down to business. "Mr. Parker, I want you to tell us what happened out there when your wife got gored by that bull."

"Well, it'd done already happened when I looked between them logs into the stall. When I seen she was dead, I got scared and away I run. I was aiming to go to Canada or Mexico or somewheres like that, but Joppa, Illinoise, is as far as I got. I didn't take no money with me and I had to get a job or go hungry. Root hog or die, you might say."

"Joppa ain't on the way to Mexico, Mr. Parker, and your wife ain't dead. She's been telling the law all about how you pushed her into that stall and locked the door behind her and laughed at her while Popeye was trying to gore her to death."

"She ain't dead? No shit?"

"No shit."

"She's a damn liar then, just like she always was! That bull's probably the only male critter for miles around she ain't spread her legs for!"

"Come on, now, Mr. Parker, she's sixty-something years old."

"So what?"

"So I think you're a lying sack of shit."

"You can cuss me if you want to, and me with these chains on, you brave little fucker, but I never locked that hag in that there stall. If I was to set out to kill her, I'd kill her so she'd stay dead."

"Sounds like you're sorry she ain't dead."

"I *am* sorry she ain't dead. Now she's telling lies on me and trying to get me sent to the pen."

"No sir, she's telling the whole truth and nothing but the truth, and yes sir, you *are* headed for the pen. I expect we could get the judge to go easy on you, though, if you'd just come clean. He won't like it a bit if you keep on lying about everything."

"I ain't lying about a *Got*damn thing. I just felt a-scared and free at the same time, like there was a big monkey off my back, and so I taken off for the wild blue yonder."

So much for my efforts to talk Yolk into confessing his sins. I was put out that he'd gotten the best of me, so I kept quiet for a while and decided to try something different.

When we crossed the line back into Crittenden County, I told Alton to pull into a side road and then off into a little grove of trees. I said, "Mr. Parker, I expect you'll need to take a leak before we get on into town, because it'll take a while to get you processed. Mr. Watkins here can walk you over yonder and take your cuffs and shackles off for you."

We got him out of the car, and I said to Alton, "Uncuff him and take him over there and face him towards that open field and take his leg shackles off."

Yolk looked at me and raised one eyebrow, then shuffled along with Alton. I opened the trunk of the car and took out my rifle and chambered a round. When Yolk heard me throw the cocking lever he stopped right where he was and unbuttoned his britches and urinated. Then he looked back at me and said, "I ain't fixing to try to excape, but if you want to shoot me now you'll be doing me a big favor. What I *ain't* gonna do, no way in hell, is admit to something I never done. So make up your mind, hotshot."

I know when I'm beat. I wasn't going to shoot him anyway, so I put the rifle back in the trunk and hollered at Alton to bring Yolk on back to where I was standing so we could get him chained up and put back in the car. When we slammed the car door, Alton said, "Mr. Taylor, give me a pair of wire pliers and walk around that curve in the road there for a few minutes, and then when you come back this old peckerwood will tell you anything you want to know, including how he kidnapped the Lindbergh baby."

"I appreciate it, Alton, but I don't think so."

"It wouldn't take but about one fingernail, and he'd sing like a tweety bird."

"I reckon not. Let's go."

So we took Yolk on to jail, but before the Commonwealth of Kentucky could put him on trial he got hold of a wire coat hanger and hung himself in his cell. For some reason I felt bad when I heard about it. I couldn't decide if he killed himself because he was guilty or because he was innocent. His wife made a complete recovery and sold the farm and moved to Detroit to live with her sister. Popeye the bull got turned into dog food.

I didn't shoot Yolk Parker while he was trying to "escape" for the simple reason that I didn't know for sure he needed killing. But there was another fellow in Crittenden County who really did have it coming and I was eager to give it to him.

CHAPTER 33

WE INTERRUPT THIS
PROGRAM . . .

My Cardinals were scuffling with the Dodgers and the Boston Braves for first place in the National League. Patrolling the side roads early one morning, I was twiddling the dial on the car radio in an effort to find a St. Louis station that would give the baseball scores from the previous evening. I located the St. Louis station all right, but here's what the announcer was saying:

We interrupt this broadcast to bring you an important news bulletin.

Five men were killed and two wounded last night in a wild shootout at a Southern Illinois dairy farm.

Official sources declined to identify the wounded men, who are agents of the U. S. Treasury Department, but the same sources confirmed that the farm was allegedly a front for a criminal conspiracy to distribute untaxed whiskey in upstate urban areas.

One of the wounded agents was treated and released at a local hospital and the other has been transported to an unidentified hospital here in St. Louis. No word yet on the identity of the men who were killed.

We'll keep you posted.

And now, back to sports.

When I heard that report on the shootout down in Little Egypt, I thought back to something Mr. Burl C. Appling had said, not so long ago: *"Me and Doughball aim to locate, and then catch or kill the people responsible. Between you and me, we think that killing 'em would be the best remedy."*

It didn't take a genius to see that the shootout described on the radio had Mr. Burlap's and Doughball McKelvey's hoofprints all over it.

CHAPTER 34

THE MYSTERIOUS MURDER OF EDDIE RAY BLANKENSHIP

Hon, what if I get you a new hat for your birthday?" Irene had said. "The one you're wearing's older than you are."

I couldn't tell her I didn't *want* a new hat. I was happy with my comfortable old fedora, but I didn't want to hurt her feelings so I said, "That sounds great, baby."

She ended up buying me a wide-brimmed cattleman's hat that made me look like a walking mushroom, and I didn't have any choice but to marvel at it and wear it to work that evening. My plan was to patrol for a few hours, making sure a bunch of people saw me, and then pop by the Marion Flour Mill later on so I could give myself a special birthday treat.

The geography of the area around the mill is important because of what happened that night, and it's best explained by its relationship to the railroad tracks. A fast freight highballing through Marion would blow for the crossings at Depot Street and Highway 120, and then it would enter a sharp right-hand curve that would take it on to all points east. The flour mill was nestled in the inside of the curve to the right of the railway, and the Crackshin neighborhood was scattered at the foot of the high embankment on the left side. When negotiating the curve, the locomotive engineer could almost look right into Mr. Coleman's office window and the fireman could, if he had a good arm, throw a chunk of coal and hit Old Man Blankenship's house down in Crackshin.

At about ten minutes past eleven that night, the murderer Eddie Ray Blankenship pulled his automobile into the driveway of his family's residence and got out to go inside. He was unsteady on his feet. As he started toward his front door I stepped out of the shadows, wearing my brand-new birthday hat, and shot him once in the back of his greasy head. He collapsed on the cinders in his own front yard, dead or dying, and I fired four more quick shots into his head and threw the pistol out into the street.

I unwrapped a bandanna handkerchief from around my shooting hand, put the handkerchief in my pocket, and stepped back into the shadows and counted to five. Then I drew my own .45 automatic and ran toward Mulberry Street, shouting, "Halt or I'll shoot! Halt! Halt!" As I turned left onto Mulberry Street, I threw my hat on the ground and fired a "warning" shot straight up into the air. I turned to the left on 120 and ran back up the railroad embankment and on down the tracks toward Depot Street. Again I yelled, "Halt! Halt!" and, taking careful aim, I fired a shot straight down the southbound tracks. Then, breathing hard, I turned around and walked back the way I'd come.

As I got back to the intersection of Mulberry and 120, I flagged down a Marion city police car that was responding to the shots-fired call. The night hack was Virgil Oliver. I leaned into the open window of the passenger door and said, "Virgil, I was up at the mill and I heard some shots and came down the embankment and saw somebody laying in one of the yards with another fellow standing over him. He ran around the block here, and then down the tracks toward the depot and I chased him. I fired a shot at him up on the tracks, but I don't think I hit him."

"Get in. I better get on up to the scene."

"I need to look for my hat. I lost it along here somewhere and I'd better grab it if we see it. My wife just gave it to me for my birthday."

"Don't want you to be in trouble with the old lady," Virgil said. He spotted the hat and pulled over so I could jam it back on my head. When he and I drove up to the crime scene, we saw that a small crowd had gathered around Eddie Ray's body. From the street you couldn't tell who it was lying there. Eddie Ray's mother and one of his dumpy sisters were hugging each other and howling, and Old Man Blankenship was standing in the yard, drunk, barefooted, and bewildered. My blood was up and I found myself wishing there was some way I could kill him too, but there wasn't any convenient way to do it.

Several neighbors were interested parties to the spectacle, including a lantern-jawed woman in a pink housecoat. Virgil said to her, "Mrs. Murphy, do you know what happened?"

"Not for sure. I was asleep with the winder open and I heard some shots and hollering, and then some more shots farther away. I thought it was firecrackers, but it must've been gunshots, cause there lays a fellow that's done been shot." Virgil looked at me and rolled his eyes as the woman rattled on. "Which one of 'em is it? It's one of the Blankenship boys, ain't it?" She craned her neck to get a better view.

"I don't know, ma'am, that's what I'm here to find out," Virgil said. "Would you please go inside and call Chief Fielder and tell him what happened and ask him to come on over here? I can't think of his home number, but you can just ask the operator to ring him."

As the neighbor lady ambled off to do as she was told, a buck-toothed teenager rushed up to Virgil, waving a small blue-steel revolver. "Looky what I found over yonder by that telephone pole!" he cried.

Virgil was outraged. "God damn you, don't point that thing at me! Gimme it!" He looked at me triumphantly and said, "This must be the murder weapon."

I shrugged. I'd been standing right by the police car because it wasn't my place as a county deputy to interfere in the city police investigation of this apparent homicide. When Chief of Police R. B. Fielder arrived at the scene, I gave him a brief account of my version of the incident. I offered to write out a statement while my memory was still fresh, and the chief agreed that was a good idea. So without another look at the dead body and the grieving family, I climbed back up the embankment and crossed the tracks and went and locked up the mill. Then I drove to City Hall where I found a child's school tablet and sat down to write my report:

To R. B. Fielder, Chief of Police:

I own an interest in the Marion Flour Mill from my father's will. Arrived there about 10:30 p.m. on 8 June 1948 and reviewed some accounts in the office. Afterwards, I went out back to smoke. I had just lit up and taken a seat on the old loading dock when I saw the lights of a car pulling into a driveway down in Crackshin. I now believe it was one of the Blankenship boys, but I am not sure which one. At the time, I had no idea who it was.

Heard a shot, then more shots, don't know how many for sure, maybe 3 or 4. I ran down there and saw a man standing over a body and he took off running and I chased him out of Crackshin and down Mulberry Street and then back around and down the tracks towards the depot. I was hollering for him to stop, and I fired a warning shot somewhere on Mulberry and another shot for effect while on the tracks. Probably didn't hit him because he didn't slow down any.

I ran nearly to Depot Street and gave out. Last saw suspect going past the depot, then out of sight. White man, medium build, dark shirt and pants, couldn't see the color of his eyes or hair.

Respectfully,
E. O. Taylor, Deputy

CHAPTER 35

INTERVIEW WITH CHIEF FIELDER

After completing the written report, I drove home and went to bed, but I didn't sleep a wink. I was a little too keyed up. I hadn't killed anybody since I greased that Russian rapist in Berlin, and there's really nothing quite like a good homicide to get your blood to pumping. I was hopped up like a dope fiend.

Next morning, Jess telephoned to say that Chief Fielder wanted to talk to me about my role in last night's exciting events. Jess was upset that I hadn't called him.

"Gene, it was embarrassing when he called me and I didn't know what the hell he was talking about. You could've let me know."

"It wasn't sheriff's business, it was city police business. What does R. B. want with me? I wrote it all down for him last night."

"I don't know. What have you been up to? Do we need to get you a lawyer?"

"No."

"Do you want me to go with you when you talk to him?"

"No."

"Well, he'd like to see you uptown at one this afternoon."

"I'll be there," I said, and hung up the phone.

Later that day, I walked into City Hall and found R .B. chewing on one end of his stringy white mustache and pecking at an old Underwood typewriter. His hands were so big the machine looked like a toy. When he saw me, he held up a frankfurter-sized forefinger indicating that I should let him finish what he was doing. He typed a few final strokes and then got up and motioned me into a chair. He wore a white shirt and blue uniform trousers and his sidearm appeared to be an old-time Smith & Wesson military revolver, one of those with a lanyard ring screwed into the butt. I shook hands with him and said, "Jess said you wanted to see me."

"That's right. Thanks for coming by. I've been a busy man since I seen you last. I might as well tell you, the Blankenships think you're the fellow who killed their boy."

"Well, I didn't. Which boy was it anyway? Nobody ever told me."

"It was Eddie Ray, the youngest one."

"I never knew him very well."

"Some people are saying it's odd you happened to be so close by when it happened."

"I believe I explained that in my report."

"You did, and I've already been around to see Blinky Coleman to check on what you said. He says you've been in and out of there at night for the past two or three months. He showed me some notes you and him have wrote back and forth. I don't think he thinks you've got very good sense."

"He's not the only one who thinks that."

"Anyway, I went out back on that old dock and found a sand bucket with a whole bunch of cigarette butts in it. What brand is it you smoke?"

I held up a pack of Lucky Strikes.

"I found one cigarette that looked like it'd been stubbed out right after it was lit. Was you smoking when you heard the shots down at the Blankenships' house?" R. B. was taking notes with a lead pencil.

"I'd just lit a cigarette when I heard shots from down below the embankment in Crackshin. At the time, I didn't know they came from the Blankenships' place."

"And so what'd you do?"

"I guess I stubbed out the cigarette, I don't remember, and I jumped off the dock and crossed the tracks and went down the embankment. I remember I nearly busted my ass when I tripped over a root or something. When I got to the bottom I saw this guy standing beside what looked like a body laying there in that yard. When he saw me he lit out for Mulberry Street."

"Did he have a gun in his hand?"

"I didn't see one. I figured he had one, though, because of the shots I heard. I believe that's what the detectives call a clue."

R.B. ignored my clever remark and took a moment to sharpen his pencil with a yellow-handled Case pocketknife. "Did you hear Eddie Ray say anything?"

"I didn't know it was Eddie Ray till you just now told me it was. Lights were just beginning to come on in the houses as I ran after the other guy, and all I could see when I ran past was a stiff laying there in the yard. I didn't hear anything else except my own breathing and my feet hitting the ground as I was running."

"Did you holler at this guy and tell him to stop?"

"I hollered and I also fired a warning shot after I turned the corner onto Mulberry Street. My hat blew off about the time I fired that first shot. It's a new hat my wife bought me. Virgil can tell you where it was and you can probably find the cartridge casing from the shot I fired, if you haven't found it already."

"What did he look like?"

"Who, Virgil?"

"No, the guy you *say* you was chasing."

"Just like I described him in my report. I wouldn't know him if he walked through that door."

"You never did see a gun?"

"Well, I had my .45, but I never saw a gun on the guy I chased. Some squirrel-toothed kid found a little revolver after I went back up there with Virgil. You'll be lucky to get any prints off of it, though, after him and Virgil wallowed it around."

"I sent it off to the state lab this morning."

"Good luck on that. Do you have other questions?"

"Just a couple more. I remember when your dad killed the oldest Blankenship boy back in '35. Do you think any of his family might've been in on his murder last year?"

"The idea came up when my brothers and I were trying to figure out who killed him. We sort of wrote them off as suspects, though. Jess says they don't have enough ambition to kill anybody, and I reckon he's right."

"So none of you all have got any big grudge against the Blankenships?"

"I don't hold any grudges. *Forgive and forget* is my motto, but you'd have to ask Mom and Jess and Hack if they harbor vengeful feelings. I will tell you that the old man pissed me off a right smart when I went around to talk to him after Dad was murdered. He spoke disrespectful about my mother and I told him to shut his mouth, or words to that effect."

R. B. nodded and said, "Well, I guess we'll just have to keep looking for the killer. Maybe we'll find him or maybe he'll get to feeling guilty about it and come in and confess."

I looked him in the eye and said, "Don't bet the farm on it."

I was walking back to my car, when I heard a voice I recognized: "Hey there, Jellybean."

Yes, it was Burl C. Appling himself, sitting alone on the covered open-air bandstand there on the front corner of the courthouse square. He had a bandage over his left eye and another one over his left ear and several band-aids on the left side of his neck.

"Hello, Mr. Burlap," I said. "What got ahold of you?"

"Ain't you been listening to the news?"

"Nah, about all I listen to are the farm reports and the baseball scores. The rest of it depresses me."

So Mr. Burlap proceeded to tell me how he and Doughball McKelvey had finally put together a network of Illinois informants who pointed them toward a rural enterprise called the Little Egypt Dairy. The owner of the dairy was a man named Joseph "Irish Joe" Dullenty, formerly a resident of East St. Louis, now supposedly a big milk and butter man in Little Egypt.

Further investigation revealed that there was neither hoof nor horn nor milk-filled udder to be found anywhere on the premises of the alleged dairy, although Irish Joe did have a couple of modern reefer trucks purportedly to haul ten-gallon cans of milk, but in fact used to haul ten-gallon cans full of Kentucky ardent spirits to be distributed here and there in the Land of Lincoln.

"So what'd you do?"

"Well, me and Doughball went to a little federal judge up there and got us a search warrant for Mr. Dullenty's premises. Once we had the warrant, there was nothing left to do but go out there and serve it, so that's what we done."

"How many in your posse?"

"We didn't want no posse. Me and Doughball was a-plenty. Anyway, me and him visited the Little Egypt Dairy a couple of nights ago and, upon arrival, observed Irish Joe Dullenty and several accomplices in the act of unloading a reefer truck full of what we correctly believed to be Kentucky corn liquor."

"You sound like you're already testifying in court."

"Yeah, but this case ain't likely to ever go to court. Dullenty and his boys didn't give us no time to read the warrant or even announce ourselves as officers. Don't even know for sure they realized who we was—for all I know they thought we was high-jackers—but out they come with their pistols, which placed me and Doughball in reasonable fear of death or grievous injury."

"It didn't end well for the dairy men, did it?"

"You could say that. Doughball had the Monitor and I had a Model 8 Remington. Everybody commenced firing about the same time. I shot Dullenty full of holes and Doughball went to chugging away with the Monitor and between us we topped every single one of them jaybirds. We run the Remington and the Monitor dry and finished the fight with our sidearms."

"Sounds like you had them just ever so slightly outgunned."

"Yes, yes, I believe you could say that, but they was driving the train. They made a big mistake when they pulled on us. Between you and me, them suckers was about the worst shot-up men you ever seen. We shot 'em till they quit twitching. A couple of 'em even had bullet holes in the bottoms of their feet. Me and Doughball think if you go to all the trouble to shoot an outlaw, you don't want him getting up again when you ain't looking. Five of 'em kilt, none wounded, none missing."

"So how'd you get hurt? Are you shot?"

"No, Doughball's the one that got shot. He got hit twice—maybe by ricochets—while he was defending himself against Dullenty's boys. Myself, I got pretty near beat to death and set afire by hot .30-06 brass coming out of that damn Monitor. Why, I had to peel one empty shell off my eyebrow before it burnt my eyeball out. Son, take it from me, don't ever stand nowhere near the ejection port of a Colt Monitor when it's taking care of business."

"So tell me, how's Doughball getting along? Is he dead?"

"Nah, you can't kill that fat little Texan. He's in the hospital up in St Louis. I'm heading back up that way as soon as I finish up some business here."

"What other business?"

"Well, I need to pay a fellow a debt for helping out a friend of mine."

"I didn't know you had any friends, except for Doughball."

"Oh, me and Doughball ain't friends, we just hunt in the same pack. My friend's a young woman whose mother I used to know, and this fellow helped her get out of a bad situation."

"Are you talking about Vinita Shelton?"

"Correct. Now listen to me, we've got information from a local snitch about some people here in this county—including at least one county official—who've been in on making and selling whiskey to the late Irish Joe. But with all them dead men up there in Little Egypt there's no more market for white whiskey made on this side of the river."

"I'll take a wild guess that your snitch is Vinita's worthless father."

"Could be, but I'm in charge of this here investigation and, right now, I don't think there's enough admissible evidence to connect anybody in this county to Little Egypt, provided you hillbillies can keep your damn mouths shut. Are you following me, son?"

"Yes sir, I follow."

"In case I'm not making myself real clear, you need to tell your criminal brother, Acting Sheriff Jesse Taylor, and his criminal co-conspirators to bust up their stills and go to growing punkins or something."

"That young woman you mentioned is quite a gal."

"She had the best mama and the sorriest daddy that ever lived. She's had a hard way to go, since her mama died, but she's a tough, smart girl and she'll land on her feet. Before I leave town I'm going to pop by and have a chat with her daddy, so he won't cause her no problems on down the line."

"Glad to hear it. What are the chances Vinita might come back here one of these days and talk about some things that oughtn't to be talked about?"

"Listen, you could burn that little girl at the stake and she wouldn't squeal on anybody! Even if she knows something on you—and I, of course, have no idea what it might be, except for some suspicions Chief R.B. Fielder told me about earlier today— she also knows you helped her out and she ain't ever in a million years gonna rat on you."

"Well, that's a comfort, I guess, but I don't have any secrets for her to tell about. My life's an open book for all to see."

"Still just as honest as the day is long, ain't you, Jellybean?"

On the way home I realized all of a sudden that my body was running on empty. The muscles in my arms hurt and my back felt like somebody had worked me over with a club. When I got home I went into the front bedroom and took off my clothes and went straight to bed, even though it was only about four o'clock in the afternoon.

I immediately fell into a deep sleep and began dreaming that a bunch of German soldiers were chasing me through the woods in the snow. They cornered me and they were laughing and I woke up right before they stuck bayonets into me. I was relieved when I realized it was all just a nightmare but as soon as I went back to sleep, here they came again.

This time I couldn't wake up and make them stop, and after a while a Tiger tank got after me and I could hear men screaming from inside the tank. The Tiger swerved and its tread was about to run over me and I couldn't move out of the way and the men in the tank were screaming louder and louder like they were burning alive, but they weren't.

"Hey, hey, hey." Irene was talking to me from the side of the bed. She knew better than to touch me when I was having a nightmare. I woke up breathing hard and streaming with sweat. The sheet and the pillow case were soaked.

"What time is it?"

"About a quarter till ten. Do you want some supper?"

"No, I just want to sleep." She made me get up so I could get a dry pair of pajamas and she could change the bedclothes, then tucked me back in and climbed into bed beside me. I rolled over and curled up and she fitted her big belly against my back and legs and wrapped her arms around me, and after a while I went back to sleep.

I didn't wake up again till way in the night. Irene was sleeping peacefully beside me and I had kicked all my bedcovers off. I was chilled from the night breeze that was coming through the open windows of the bedroom, so I pulled the sheet up all the way over my head and shivered there in the dark. A whippoorwill was calling from somewhere in the front yard, but his cry was harsh, more like a dog barking than a birdcall. He hushed his noise when an owl started sounding off from the hollow down below the house.

Who, who, who cooks for you? said the owl. *Who, who, who cooks for you all?*

CHAPTER 36

JUNE 1948:
JAMES GAVIN TAYLOR

The three hired men and I had been working hard, cleaning and fixing and painting, so Mom fed all of us our noon meal at the big house. Afterwards, she said, "Why don't you all go out and sit on the front porch in the shade and relax while I just finish up the dishes? Here's the *Courier-Journal* and the *Times* you can look at. The birth announcement's in the *Times*."

"Yes, ma'am," said Shad and Shack in unison, and they clumped through the house and out onto the porch, followed by Bob Martin and me.

I found the birth announcement in the local paper and read it to myself: *Born, on June 19, at the Crittenden County Hospital to Mr. and Mrs. E. O. Taylor, a son, James Gavin Taylor.* After a couple of minutes, I handed the paper to Shack Westmoreland, who read the announcement and shook his head.

"It's a shame Ross never lived to see this baby," Shack said. "Why didn't you all name it after him, anyhow? What kind of a name's Gayvin?"

"It's Gavin, not Gayvin. He was an officer I worked for during the war."

"Well, did everybody get enough to eat?" Mom asked brightly, as she came through the door and took a seat in the porch swing.

"Yes, ma'am, Miss Lera, we're full as ticks. We shore are proud about the new baby. Do you all know when he'll be coming home?"

"Tomorrow or the next day, I imagine," Mom said. "Dr. Faulkner wants to make sure Irene's okay first. It was a hard birth and she had to have some stitches, you know, because that baby came in a hurry."

The three old bachelors blushed and looked away into the distance. They didn't know how to respond to such an intimate disclosure. Finally Shad said, "Well . . . uh . . . I guess you all are awful happy." To change the subject, he reached over and slapped my knee, "We're expecting cigars from you, Pappy Gene, and not cheap ones neither."

"Aw, a cigar'd make you sick," Shack said. "Better get him some bon bons instead, Gene."

Bob had finished looking at the Louisville paper and he handed it to me, indicating by a glance that I should read a certain article that proved to be of local interest:

CRITTENDEN MURDER BAFFLES POLICE

Local and state authorities say they still have no leads in solving the brutal murder of Eddie Ray Blankenship, 31, of Marion. Blankenship, was shot five times in the head with a small revolver, which the murderer dropped before he fled down the Illinois Central right of way.

The murder weapon has been carefully examined in the state crime laboratory, but state experts are apparently unable to collect any useful fingerprint evidence. Speaking on condition of anonymity, an official at the lab told this newspaper that the weapon is an older model Iver Johnson revolver, sometimes called an 'Owl Head,' from a design molded into the pistol's hard rubber grips. Our informant says that thousands of these inexpensive revolvers were made, primarily in .32 and .38 calibers, and it is therefore unlikely that ownership of the weapon can be traced.

As I digested this news, it occurred to me that Chief of Police R. B. Fielder—a wise old rat around the barn if there ever was one—probably had a pretty good idea who blew Eddie Ray Blankenship's brains out. But the only people who could offer any circumstantial evidence connecting me with the mysterious murder of Eddie Ray Blankenship were Old Man Bob Martin and bad-girl Vinita Shelton.

I was one hundred percent certain that the old man would not "remember" that he gave me a .38 Owl Head pistol, and I was ninety-nine percent certain (based on what Burl C. Appling told me) that Vinita Shelton would never disclose that she told me that Eddie Ray killed my father. Moreover, she really couldn't do that without implicating herself as an accomplice.

The fact was, Chief Fielder was never going to be able to prove my guilt without an admission from me, and no way would I ever start feeling guilty and confess to murdering Eddie Ray, and here's why: I was glad I did it! Enjoyed it, in fact, and wished I could've killed the son of a bitch three or four times instead of just once!

CHAPTER 37

AT HOME

Supper was over, the shadows long, the workday finished. Mom went off to the garden with a basket on her arm, and Irene sat on the kitchen porch snapping green beans and dropping the pieces into a dishpan. I relaxed nearby, shirtless in my work-stained overalls, holding Baby Gavin. Irene was humming to herself and I found myself thinking what a grand, lucky thing it is to sit quietly with a contented and loving wife.

As I looked into my son's little face and smelled his talcum smell, I thought about all the people, good and bad, who'd come marching down through the centuries mingling their blood to create this one little creature. I wondered what kind of man he'd grow up to be.

Dad and Jess and I were criminals, each of us in our own fashion, and I couldn't think of a single trait of mine or theirs I'd want my boy to have, unless it was Dad's ability to tell a funny story. Cortez McDowell, Irene's dad, was a good man, but I wouldn't wish his grumpy disposition on a blameless child.

There was really no doubt about it. I wanted my boy to take after the women in his family tree. Polly Tawber, the indomitable pioneer Indian woman. Aunt Susie Hughey, who stood toe-to-toe with a whole band of Rebel cutthroats. My mom, smart as a whip and tough as whet leather. Irene's mom, ever gentle and kind. And most of all, there was my Irene—my helpmeet—my treasure. Some of these women had brains; some had physical strength; some had courage; some a sweet spirit; some with all of the above. A little boy could do a lot worse.

The two heartbeats there on the porch with me were the greatest blessings the Good Lord could ever give me, even if I was a cold-blooded murderer in the eyes of the law. Little Gavin didn't know or care that bloody hands were holding him, and the only thing Irene really knew for sure was that I sometimes had bad dreams about the war. I was going to have to make the best of the rest of my life for their sakes.

I had handled a problem the Kentucky way and not the legal way, but now I could move forward and live the rest of my life here on the farm with Irene and the baby, and maybe I'd never again have a reason to raise my hand in anger against either man or beast. I'd just drift along, never look back, and hope I'd come to rest on solid ground.

ABOUT THE AUTHOR

John M. L. Brown comes from a long line of Kentuckians. He was born in Crittenden County and will be the sixth generation of his family to be buried there. He attended Vanderbilt University for both his bachelor's and JD degrees. He served in the U.S. Navy from 1970 to 1974. Since 1977, he has worked as a trial lawyer in Nashville. He lives with his wife Faye in Whites Creek, Tennessee.

Made in the USA
Monee, IL
29 November 2022

18931656R00128